Praise for *Pegasus Descending*

"Complex . . . lyrical and richly drawn." —Scott Veale, *The New York Times*

"Burke [has perfected] a seductive writing style mingling mythology, memory tales, poetic ruminations on nature, allusions mystical and Freudian, and enough criminology, melodrama, colorful patter, action, romance and ultra-violence to keep the pages turning and a reader's blood pumping."

—Dick Lochte, *Los Angeles Times*

"Never before has Burke assembled such a Dickensian array of characters. Each one is sketched visually and linguistically with captivating vividness."

—John Dugdale, *The Sunday Times* (London)

Praise for *Crusader's Cross*

"Burke's strength has long been his ability to convey both the exceptional beauty and the exceptional violence of the American South. . . . If you believe, as he does, that beauty and horror go hand in hand in this life, Burke can touch you in ways few writers can." —Patrick Anderson, *The Washington Post*

"Burke's not afraid to write beautifully about awful things. There is nothing unmanly in being erudite, in crafting sentences that almost sing, and in striving to create literature out of the muck of human cruelty." —David Granger, *Esquire*

"Burke masterfully combines landscape and memory in a violent, complex story peopled by sharply defined characters who inhabit a lush, sensual, almost mythological world." —*Publishers Weekly*

"What really draws Burke's readers in is his marvelous prose, as humid as a Gulf summer and as full of spark and menace as a thunderhead."

—*The Boston Globe*

"Burke is a genius—this novel, complex, deeply mystical and violent, is another triumph." —Joolz Denby, *The Guardian* (London)

JAMES LEE BURKE

Jesus Out to Sea
Stories

Simon & Schuster Paperbacks
New York London Toronto Sydney

Simon & Schuster Paperbacks
1230 Avenue of the Americas
New York, NY 10020

See page 241 for full information on where these stories first appeared.

First Simon & Schuster trade paperback edition July 2007

SIMON & SCHUSTER PAPERBACKS and colophon
are registered trademarks of Simon & Schuster, Inc.

For information about special discounts for bulk purchases,
please contact Simon & Schuster Special Sales at
1-800-456-6798 or business@simonandschuster.com.

Designed by Davina Mock-Maniscalco

Manufactured in the United States of America

10   9   8   7   6   5   4   3   2   1

Library of Congress Cataloging-in-Publication Data

Burke, James Lee.
Jesus out to sea : stories / James Lee Burke.
p. cm.
I. Title.
PS3552.U723J47 2007
813'.54—dc22   2006100977
ISBN-13: 978-1-4165-4856-0 (pbk)
ISBN-10:   1-4165-4856-4 (pbk)

For Paul and Muilee Pai

Contents

Jesus Out to Sea

Winter
Light

He lived alone at the head of the canyon in a two-story log house that controlled the access to the national forest area behind his property. His house was built up on a slope above a creek that flowed down from a chain of lakes high up on the plateau, and from his writing desk at his second-story window he could look out over the wide sweep of valley below and see the snow blowing out of the ponderosa on the crests of the hills and the sharply etched tracks of deer that had gone down to drink in the stream during the night. He could also see the long black scar of a road that wound its way

up from the interstate, past the one working ranch left in the valley, to the foot of his property, and finally to the public woods behind his house.

The sunlight was red on the snow, the shadows already purple in the trees, the wind colder and flecked with ice crystals against the window glass, and he knew the hunters would be there soon. They almost always came in the late afternoon, because it was only a ten-mile drive from town and with a little luck they could get in a few shots before the official close of the hunter's day thirty minutes after sunset.

He was fifty-eight and he had taken early retirement from his position as a literature professor at the university, but he had no interest in the activities of retirement or people his own age. Most of his friends were college students, and in one way or another his property always seemed marked more by their presence than his: tepee poles stacked against his toolshed, the willow-stick outline of a sweat lodge by the creek, a communal vegetable garden whose rows were now frozen into iron ridges.

A red Toyota jeep, as bright against the snow as a fire engine, ground in four-wheel drive up the road, then slowed as the driver and his passenger peered through their ice-streaked windows at the signs fastened to the trunks of larch trees at the foot of the professor's property:

THIS IS A PRIVATE ROAD

NO HUNTING

NO SHOOTING

NO TRESPASSING

But they drove on anyway, and he met them outside his door, with a cup of coffee in his hand, in his worn corduroy pants, lace-on boots, and flannel shirt. He had played basketball for LSU, and he was tall and angular, bareheaded in the wind, his skin red and coarse with the cold.

He was not unkind to them. He never was. Sometimes he invited them inside; usually they simply went away, confused or mildly irritated. But these two were different. The passenger had a dark light in his face and wore an untrimmed beard and spit regularly in the snow. His hands were square and big and seamed with dirt, and he opened and closed them impatiently. The driver was a fat man who wore three shirts that hung outside his pants, galoshes, a neon-orange hunter's vest, and a narrow skinning knife in a scabbard on his side. He smiled while he talked, but his eyes did not go with his face.

The professor, whose name was Roger Guidry, listened to the driver talk, his slender fingers wrapped around his coffee cup, his head nodding absently as he scraped at the snow with the tip of his boot. Then, when the overweight man had finished, he said, "You can walk in from the other side and hunt, if you want."

"The other side?" the driver said.

"Yes."

"How far a walk is that?"

"Fifteen miles."

"Fifteen miles," the driver said, nodding his head up and down. "Fifteen miles in snow, you're saying?"

"That's right."

"I told you we're bow hunters. We're not going to put a bullet into somebody's house or shoot somebody's cows."

"I know that."

"Listen—" the driver said.

The passenger hit him on the arm and said, "Forget it. Let's go."

"Just a minute," the driver said. "You're telling me to walk fifteen fucking miles through snow?"

"It's your choice."

"My choice?"

"That's right."

"I've heard about you."

"Oh?" Roger said.

"Yeah. I just didn't know it was this canyon."

"I see."

"We've still got time to go up the Blackfoot. Forget this guy," the passenger said.

The driver put an unlit cigarette in his mouth and looked around the yard as though he were deciding something. Then he laughed, lit his cigarette, and looked off down the valley.

"Too much," he said. Then they both got in the jeep, backed it around in the snow, cracking an old tomato stake in the vegetable garden, and crunched down the road over their own long lines of stenciled tire tracks.

The coffee cup was cold in the professor's hand. He looked down at the creek that flowed out of the dark stands of pine and fir in the national forest. In the center the riffle was a deep blue-green between sheets of ice that looked like teeth. Through the willow frame of the sweat lodge he could see two smooth, round boulders that always reminded him of a woman's breasts, and behind them a barkless and polished cottonwood that beavers had toppled into the stream to form an eddying pool whose pebbled bottom was always marbled with the shapes of cutthroat and brookie trout. In the spring and summer he and the students would fish the pool, have community dinners among the ferns on the bank, and pack far into the canyon, where the cinnamon bears and white-tailed deer were never hunted and bighorn sheep grazed through the saddles high up on the peaks.

The frozen trunks of the ponderosas creaked in the wind, powdering snow in the twilight.

In the spring, he thought.

≈≈≈

He didn't remember at which particular stage of his dissatisfaction with university life he had decided to take early retirement. Others had tried to dissuade him—he was a wonderful teacher, he would be hurt financially, he would be missed by his students. And there was truth in what they said, but he had reached the age, he told himself, when he no longer had to apologize or defend.

Maybe it had been the interminable department and committee meetings, the jealousies and hatreds that his colleagues kept alive like green wounds for decades, the self-anointed liberals whose pension plans were invested in nuclear energy, South Africa, and the Boeing Company. He tried, at least in his own mind, not to be hard on them, but in reality they filled him with a visceral disgust. There was often a sneer in their laughter, an atmosphere of bitterness and personal failure in their meeting rooms that was almost palpable, like the smell of fear. They denigrated anyone who accomplished anything and tried to sabotage any educational innovation that threatened their own meager positions. If any of them had acquired any wisdom in their years as educators, he had yet to see the instance.

No, he did remember when he made his decision to hang it up. A search committee had to meet during the Christmas holidays to choose from a huge file of applicants for a vacant position. The chair of the committee, Waldo Gates, and one of his allies, consistently gave low ratings to the most qualified candidates and high ratings to people with no publications and little experience. Waldo Gates, who lived across the creek from Roger, was also a hunter. He had even worn his mail-order camouflage fatigues and brown corduroy shooting vest to the meeting. His friend was dressed for the hunt, too, and both of them kept looking at their watches. After they had just sandbagged a Ph.D. from Stanford who had published two collections of critical essays, it was obvious to Roger that the department was about to hire an underqualified and frightened young woman who would be easily controlled by Waldo and his coterie, and Waldo and his committee ally would soon be duck-hunting at the reservoir south of town.

Waldo was sitting at the desk in the front of the room. He wore a red chin beard and horn-rimmed glasses low on his nose. His eyes were lime green, the size of dimes, and they never blinked when they looked over the top of his glasses at someone, which gave him the appearance of candor and directness and which always intimidated students and younger faculty members.

He held a file folder gingerly between his fingers and clicked it up and down on the desk. "I think we've found the lady we need here," he said. "And it seems to me we have more or less a majority agreement on that, sooooooo"—his eyes roved over the five other faces in the room, and two junior faculty members glanced away—"unless anyone else has anything to say, we can be on our way."

"Going out to make things fall down, are you?" Roger said.

"I beg your pardon," Waldo said.

"Have you guys ever thought about an open season on people? You could establish these big reserve areas enclosed by electric fences where y'all could go inside and hunt each other for, say, three or four days at a time. Blow blood, brains, and hair all over the bushes and have a fine time. Except it'd be a genuine sport because the prey would have guns, too. What do you think, Waldo?"

"I think your cause is silly and your personal life needs some attention." Waldo's eyes were round and lidless in his soft face.

"Would you care to explain that?" Roger said.

"There's life after divorce. That's why people have divorces. You end a relationship and you go on with your life. You don't lay off your problems on your colleagues."

"Maybe we could talk about that later, Waldo." Roger cleared his throat slightly. "Outside somewhere. I'll keep one hand in my pocket. In fact, I'll turn my back so the position will be more familiar for you."

"I'm glad you've gotten that off your chest, Roger. I'll report your remarks to the dean. Then you can take it up with him. I believe our committee work is done, ladies and gentlemen. Sooooooo, unless Dr. Guidry has any more entertaining observations to make, we'll say God bless and good evening."

They left him alone in the room, feeling foolish and wrong. Did he always have to speak his mind, as a child would, he thought, then spend the rest of the day rationalizing his impetuosity? He looked wistfully out the window at the brown, grassy slope of the mountain behind the campus and the thick stands of ponderosa that grew along the crest and through the saddles. The trunks were orange in the sunlight, wet with melted snow, the pine needles as dark and shiny as clusters of splintered blue glass. High up on the wind stream a hawk floated against the thin wafer of pink, winter sun.

Then Roger heard the janitor knock his broom against one of the wood desks. He picked up his briefcase at his foot, smiled politely, and walked across the empty quadrangle to his pickup truck. His vehicle was the only one in the parking lot, and for some illogical reason that fact struck him as significant.

≋

His son was away at Stanford, and his two daughters had started their own lives in Oregon and Minnesota. They came to see him in the summer, usually with friends, and their conversations were alive with subjects that seemed to exist just beyond the borders of his knowledge or his interest. After the divorce he had thought of his wife only with anger, and when the anger passed he could think of nothing except the ringing winter loneliness in his house.

Young women were available, certainly, both out of affection as well as kindness. He woke hard in the morning, throbbing with desire, and he had to sit quietly on the side of his bed in his underwear and force his mind empty of their shapes, their bare thighs and breasts, their lips, their hands that wanted to stroke his sex. But he managed to live celibate, castigating himself in the silence for his prurient thoughts, on one occasion walking far up the canyon in knee-deep snow, beating his arms in the cold, saying, "Bullshit, bullshit." A whitetail doe crisscrossed the trail in front of him, staring back at him with brown, curious eyes.

≋

The morning after the visit of the hunters in the Toyota
jeep, he walked outside into the brilliant sunlight reflecting
off the snow, the air as sharp and cold inside the lungs as
ice water, and began stacking firewood in his wheelbarrow
to take back to the house. His malamute, Boomer, who was
as big and thick through the middle as a small cinnamon
bear, frisked in the snow, snorting down in a badger hole
by the garden, pulling a stick out of the snow and throwing
it in the air.

Then Roger saw that it was not a stick, that it was made
of aluminum and the flanged steel tip was the point of a
hunter's arrow. He caught Boomer by the thick nape of skin
on the back of his neck and forced him to release the shaft
from his jaws. The point of the arrow felt as sharp as a razor
against the ball of his thumb.

It could have come from Waldo's, across the creek, he
thought. He looked through the leafless cottonwoods at the
stacked hay bales that Waldo and his children used as an
archery target. Yes yes yes, Waldo, he thought. Always
Waldo. Last summer Waldo had been bothered by a skunk
under his woodshed, and he had hired an out-of-work
sawyer to tender-trap it inside a vinyl garbage bag. The
sawyer had fitted the crimped end of the bag over his
exhaust pipe and, while Waldo watched from his window,
asphyxiated the animal to make a pair of gloves for Waldo's
oldest son.

But Roger well knew the reason for his deliberate re-
membrance of a past grievance. The arrow didn't come
from Waldo's property. Waldo was not a bow hunter, and

also the trajectory of the arrow was almost straight down, which meant that it had not bounced off the top of a hay bale and flown across the creek but instead had been fired high into the air so that it would drop cleanly into Roger's yard.

It could have fallen out of their jeep when their doors were opened, he told himself. It could have happened that way. Yes. But he felt his heart clicking against his ribs.

≈≈≈

The next day was bright and clear and windless, and the valley was white and dazzling under a bluebird sky. By afternoon, the sun was so warm that the snow had begun to pock in the fields and melt around the base of the ponderosa trunks. All day he waited for them to return. But when the sun finally dropped behind the pines on the valley's western rim and the snowfields turned as purple as a bruise, only one vehicle had come up the county road, Waldo's, carrying Waldo and a graduate teaching assistant, a statuesque blond girl named Gretchen whom Waldo had requested as his grader.

Two days later, right at daybreak, he heard a four-wheel-drive transmission grinding up the road, and when he looked through his window, his breath clouding against the glass, he saw the red Toyota jeep stop at the foot of his property. The two hunters got out with shotguns and empty canvas backpacks, cut through the bare cottonwoods, stepped gingerly across the boulders in the creek, and threaded their way through fences, brush, trees, and an abandoned horse corral at the back of Waldo's property until they reached the trail that led into the national forest.

In minutes he heard their shotguns booming. He put on his glasses and found Waldo's telephone number in the directory. The phone rang a dozen times before Waldo picked up the receiver, his voice full of sleep.

"Waldo, two guys just went through the back of your property," Roger said.

"What guys? What are you talking about?"

"Two hunters. I wouldn't let them into the canyon, so they crossed the creek and climbed through your fences."

"What do you want me to do about it?"

"You want guys with shotguns walking by your back door without permission?"

"So when you see them, tell them to ask. In the meantime I don't appreciate your waking me up because of your personal problem with hunting. Get some help, Roger, because you're an ongoing pain in the ass."

The line went dead, and Roger looked out at the blueness of the morning, the black, leafless shapes of the cottonwoods along the creek bank, heard the deep, booming echo of another shotgun blast up the canyon, and felt the cold pierce his naked feet like nails.

Two hours later the hunters walked out of the canyon in full sunlight, crunching through the sheath of ice and frozen snow along the creek's edge, their canvas packs fat with dead grouse. The driver, who still wore a skinning knife and galoshes that flopped on his feet, flipped a cigarette across the stream onto Roger's property, but neither he nor the other man, who had an untrimmed beard and a bitten look in his face, ever glanced in Roger's direction. Their tracks were jagged in the crusted snow. He heard one of the hunters laugh just before the driver started the jeep engine and ground the transmission into gear as sharply as Coke-bottle glass breaking.

That afternoon he drove into town and bought a forty-foot length of chain, a huge iron bolt and nut, and a Yale lock with two keys. A mile below his property, far down on the county road where he had no legal right to block access to the national forest, he looped one end of the chain around a ponderosa trunk, bolted the links together against the bark, strung the rest of the chain across the road, and locked it to a steel eyelet on an old U.S. Forest Service sign-post. Now the only other way to reach the national forest was down Waldo's private road, and Waldo had a locked, electronic gate across his cattle guard.

The only neighbors who would be affected by the chain across the county road were a hippie carpenter and his girl-friend who lived just below Roger's place. Roger stopped by their log house, drank a cup of coffee with them, and gave them one of the keys to the padlock. While he explained the reason for the chain, the carpenter and his girl-friend smiled and nodded and rolled joints out of a bowl of reefer on top of a redwood table, and he realized that they were not really listening because they considered his behavior as conventional and expected as their own.

That night, under a full moon that lighted the valley

floor like a white flame, he walked down the road in the silence, the soles of his boots squeaking on the snow, and
looked at the chain strung between the ponderosa trunk
and the signpost. He lifted it up in his palm and bounced it
against its tension. The links were heavy and cold and shiny
with ice. They felt solid and good in his hand, the way the
handle of a weapon probably did to some men. He let the
chain slip off his fingers and rock clinking back and forth in
the shadows. Far down the valley he could see the glow of
headlights from the interstate highway against the clouds.

The season was almost over, he thought. Maybe they
would not be back again this year. Maybe the birds had
been enough for their pride.

But he knew it wasn't finished yet. They had found each
other, right here, at the end of this valley, and they knew it
and so did he.

Late the next afternoon he looked out his window and saw
Gretchen, Waldo's grader, stepping carefully on the icy
stones in the creek, her arms stretched out for balance,
crossing onto his property. The wind was blowing, and her
face was red with cold and there were ice crystals in her
blond hair. When he opened the door for her, her breath
puffed up in a cloud of steam.

"The power went out, and I can't get the generator
started," she said.

Her eyes were blue and wide and the wind had made

tears in them. He closed the door behind her. Her lug boots and the bottom of her blue jeans were caked with snow.

"Where's Waldo?" he said.

"He went up to the Cabin for a drink."

"What are you doing at his house, Gretchen?"

"He just gave his midterms. He likes me to grade them close by so I can ask him questions if I have to."

Roger had known her since she had entered the English program five years ago. Her father had been a gypo logger who had been killed felling trees over in Idaho, and she lived with her mother in a clapboard house out by the pulp mill, where on a windless day the sweet-sour stench of processed pulp hung in the air like ripe sewage. She worked hard and did well in conventional classes in which the professor rewarded a student's ability to memorize, but she never took creative writing courses, and one way or another she avoided studying with professors whose ideas were eccentric or unpredictable, except for Roger, and he believed she enrolled in his courses only because he never gave anyone a grade lower than C.

"Where's Waldo's wife?" he said.

"She's out of town."

"Are the kids by themselves?"

"They went with her."

"I see. Well," he said, veiling his eyes, "let me turn off the stove and we'll get that generator started."

"We don't have to. He'll be back pretty soon. I can just wait here, can't I?"

"Sure."

"I mean, he won't be long."

"Don't worry about it. Come on upstairs and have some soup with me."

Her rear was tight against her blue jeans when she walked up the steps ahead of him. She took off her sheep-lined coat and hung it on a hook by the wood-burning stove that Roger had made out of an oil drum. Her breasts rose up high against her sweater, and Roger had to look away from her.

"Waldo told his American lit class that Ronald Reagan will probably one day be considered a near-great president," she said.

Roger was silent.

"Some of them put it in their exam papers," she said.

"Ignore it."

"What do you think, I mean about Reagan being near great?"

"I'm retired, Gretchen. I try not to think anymore about what Waldo has to say. Let me get you some soup."

"No, I can do it. I'll fix it for both of us. I'll make coffee, too, if that's all right."

He watched her at the stove, the way her sweater tightened against her back, the thickness of her hair against her neck, her large farm-girl hands.

"What's a P-38?" she asked.

"A World War Two airplane."

"No. Waldo's little boy said his daddy wore a P-38 on a chain around his neck."

"It's a GI can opener."

"Was he in the war or something?" she said.

"No, and neither was Ronald Reagan. Listen, Gretchen, this is important to understand. These kinds of men vicariously revise their lives through the suffering of others. Look, I don't want to tell you what to think or whom you should listen to . . ." He stopped and looked down at the backs of his hands. "I'm sorry," he said.

"You don't like him because he hunts animals, do you? At least that's what he thinks."

"What do you say we eat?"

Her eyes roamed over his face. He felt himself swallow. She widened her eyes and the blue in them intensified, and for just a moment his vanity almost allowed him to believe he was still attractive to a beautiful young woman and his heart raced in his chest in a way that it should not have.

Then he saw her cheeks color and her hand falter on the coffeepot. "What is it?" he asked.

Her gaze reached out the window, out over the short pines and the frozen creek toward Waldo's house. "He said he pulled a muscle carrying firewood. He said it throbbed all night and he couldn't sleep. He was standing behind me in the study while I was grading papers, and he had a tube of Ben-Gay in his hand."

Roger looked away from her face and the shine in her eyes.

"He took off his shirt and sat down next to me. He said, 'You won't mind putting just a little bit across my shoulders, will you?' "

"Gretchen, you don't have to confess anything to me—"

"While I put it on him, he kept saying I was a good girl. He said it over and over."

"I want you to forget this. You're a fine person. You don't have anything to be ashamed of. Just don't go out to Waldo's house again. Do your work at the office. If Waldo makes another overture toward you, report it to the dean. I'll back you up."

"Am I a weak person? Is that why it was me instead of somebody else?"

"No, you're brave to work and go to school. You're brave to put up with the deviousness of older people," he said, and slipped his arms around her, knowing he shouldn't, knowing that his judgment and control were coming undone now.

He could feel the wetness of her face against his throat. The thickness in his loins made him close his eyes and hold his breath so he would not see the gold down on the taper of her neck or smell the perfume in her hair.

≋

The chain did not stop them the next morning. They simply drove around it, cracking over the ice, flattening the tree saplings along the creek bank. Then just before they reached Roger's property, they veered across the creek, scouring deep black tracks along the banks, and bounced over the rocks until they reached Waldo's horse lot and access to the national forest. Roger watched through the window as they unloaded a child's sled out of the Toyota's back. The snowfields danced with light, and the plumes from the hunters' mouths were thick and white in the windless air. Then Waldo came out of his back door in a nylon vest, with a battered cowboy hat on his head, and the three men talked like old friends, laughing at something funny, looking in the direction of Roger's house. The hunters had brought scoped rifles this time, and they wore them on shoulder straps and kept shifting the guns' weight on their backs as they talked. They shook hands with Waldo and pulled their sled on a rope up into a heavy green stand of pines in the national forest.

That afternoon the valley was sealed from rim to rim with snow clouds, then a heavy white mist moved across the valley floor until the trees on the hills disappeared inside it. The rick fences and stone walls became as white as the fields, and the creek was recognizable only by a thin electric-blue riffle running through the ice. Thunder boomed through the valley, and when he heard an explosion echo off the cliff walls in the public woods, he tried to tell himself that it was only more thunder.

For some reason, that afternoon, for the first time in his life, he wondered what it would be like to kill someone. He remembered a graduate student he had taught back in the 1960s, a studious but strange kid with myopic, close-set eyes who had probably fried an element or two in his brain with LSD and once told Roger he had spent a morning in the shadows behind his second-floor apartment window, looking through the telescopic sights of an empty rifle at the passersby on the street. When Roger tried and failed to get the boy to see the campus psychologist, he wondered if the acid had inculcated such a sick urge in the boy's head or if it had simply liberated it.

Just before sunset, the sky started to clear and a mauve-colored glow filled the trees on the valley's eastern rim. Roger let Boomer outside, then a few minutes later went outside himself with a propane torch to unfreeze a water line. He saw the hunters come out of the woods on the other side of the creek, dragging their sled across the glazed slickness of the snow. The doe lashed to the sled was so enormous and heavy that both men had to pull on the rope to get the sled up the incline to their jeep. They had already gutted her, and the slit from between her back legs to her throat looked like a long strip of red silk ribbon.

He moved the white-blue flame of the propane torch up and down the water pipe and tried not to look at them as they tied down the doe on the jeep's fender. But when enough time had passed for them to have closed their doors and started their engine and he had heard only silence, he looked up and saw them sharing a drink from a chrome flask, watching him.

He shut off the valve on the propane torch and went back inside, stamping the crust of mud and snow off his boots, the propane bottle hot in his clenched hand. Their jeep ground across Waldo's property and along the frozen edges of the creek, and finally he could not hear it any-more. Then he heard a solitary rifle shot, a sharp, loud crack that meant it was not an echo, that the muzzle had been pointed in the direction of his property.

He opened the front door. It was so quiet outside he could hear a lump of snow fall through the branches of a fir tree. Boomer lay on the creek bank, a pooling dark red hole in the side of his neck, his mouth opened stiffly against the ice. The wind blew patterns in the fur along the edge of his stomach.

Roger had bought the knife for eight dollars through a mail-order service that advertised in the family magazine in the Sunday newspaper. It was made in Taiwan and copied after the pattern of the Marine Corps K-Bar. It had a ball compass inserted in the end of the tooled grip, saw teeth and a blood groove on the blade, and a honed edge that could cut weightlessly through paper.

He knew that they would stop at the Cabin up on the highway. It was the hunters' place, it was Waldo's place, where they drank busthead boilermakers at the bar, rolled the dice out of a leather cup for the drinks, and slammed the butt of their pool cues down on the floor after each shot. He didn't know why he was so sure they would be there (maybe it was the memory of a convict-student at Deer Lodge who had told Roger, "You see, Doc, right after a score you always go to a bar or a hot-pillow joint. A guy's got to share the feel of it, you know what I mean?"), and so when he came out on the highway and saw their jeep in the parking lot of the bar, the only unexpected moment of recognition was the fact that among all the pickups and cars in the lot, they had parked one vehicle away from Waldo's Power Ram.

He stepped up on the wood porch and opened the door partway. A fire burned in a hearth beyond the pool table and a flat layer of cigarette smoke hung in the purple and orange neon haze over the long, railed bar. The two hunters were eating steaks at a table, their elbows pointed outward as they sliced meat away from the bone.

Roger's hand rested lightly on top of the big knife inside his coat pocket, the blade cold and hard under his fingers. He looked at the two hunters, and in his mind, for just a moment, he saw a series of images like blisters popping across the surface of the brain: his own shape moving quickly across the barroom floor, the backhanded slash of the blade across a cheekbone, across the back of a fat neck, the genuine horror and fear in their eyes. But he felt both foolish and stupid now, and he closed the door and stepped back off the porch into the parking lot. The doe's head hung downward off the jeep's fender onto the front bumper, her eyes like brown glass in the starlight. He lifted on the tension of the nylon rope that bound her to the fender, sawed through it with the survival knife, and hefted her weight up on his shoulders. Her body had already stiffened in the cold, and her hair felt like bristles against his neck.

After he dropped her in the bed of his pickup truck, he walked back to the jeep, cut off the air stems of all four tires, then unscrewed the gas cap and systematically scooped up five handfuls of dirt and poured them into the tank.

As he pulled out onto the highway and skidded slightly on a strip of black ice, he heard an outraged voice behind him and saw in his rearview mirror the silhouettes of men filing quickly out the front door of the bar.

The vault of sky over the valley was bursting with constellations and the moon had risen high above the ponderosas and lighted the snowfields and the skeletal shapes of the cottonwoods along the creek as brightly as a phosphorous flare. He stopped his truck at the chain stretched across the road, unlocked it and let it drop clinking to the road, then drove across it and kept going through his own property until he reached the wooden gate that gave onto the national forest. From the toolbox in the bed of his truck he took a GI entrenching tool, screwed the adjustable blade into the position of a hoe, lifted the belly of the doe across his shoulders, and with her four legs gathered together across his chest, worked his way up the trail into the darkness of the forest, under the towering gray and pink cliffs that were filmed with ice in the moonlight.

He hadn't gone far when he heard the surge of a truck engine up his private road. He looked back down the trail and saw Waldo's Power Ram, with three men in the cab, stop in his yard, and behind them the headlights of cars and other pickups. He set the doe down in a tangle of huckleberry bushes and began chopping through the snow and frozen dirt with the shovel. There was no time to build a fire to thaw the ground, and with his bare hands he ripped away slabs of ice and frozen root systems that were meshed as hard as cable in the earth, felt his skin tear, a fingernail fold back on itself; then on his knees he chopped even harder into the dirt until he was down past the freeze line and the blade of the shovel bit into the moist subsoil.

He hollowed out the hole deeper, flinging humus and dirt out to the sides, then pushed the doe into it and pressed the stiffness of her flat against the contours of the earth. As he scraped the snow and leaves back over her stomach and flanks, he saw blood on the wooden shaft of the entrenching tool, and in the heart-stopping urgency of the moment he did not know if it was the doe's or his own.

The wind blew down the canyon, and the ice crystals in the larch and ponderosa pine and fir trees glittered as though in a fantasy and rang as loudly as crystal. His face was white and shining with sweat in the moon's glow.

≈≈≈

In Roger's front yard, Waldo and the hunters moved in a circle, massing their energies, their voices melding together with the sound of their truck and car engines, their shadows on the snow like simian figures moving about on a prehistoric savannah.

"We're here," one of the hunters yelled to the others. "We're here."

The

Village

had thirty guys strung out on the trail in the dark. It sounded like a traveling junkyard. I stopped them at the river, told the translator, Look, we got a problem here, two more klicks we're in Pinkville South, know what I'm saying? We go in, make our statement, then boogie on back across the river, the beer is five hours colder, and we let the dudes from Amnesty International count up the score. In and out, that's the rhythm. None of our people get hurt, even the volunteers we took out of the last ville don't need to walk through any toe-poppers.

I'm talking to guys here who think the manual of arms is a Nicaraguan baseball player.

Look, ace, you got to understand, I didn't target the ville, it targeted itself. They were giving food to the people who were killing us. We warned them, we warned the American priest running the orphanage. Nobody listened. I didn't have no grief with the Mennonite broad. I saw her in the city once, I tipped my hat to her. I admired her. She was a homely little Dutch wisp of a thing working in a shithole most people wouldn't take time to spit on. The trouble came from a couple of liaison guys, officers who spent some time at a special school for greasers at Benning. Listen, chief, I was an adviser, got me? I didn't get paid for interfering. You see these guys walk a dude into a tin shed that's got a metal bed frame in it, they close the door behind them, you'll hear the sounds way out in the jungle and pretend it's just monkeys shrieking.

Ellos! they'd yell when we came into the ville, and then try to hide. That was our name. As far as these poor bastards knew, I could have been Pancho Villa or Stonewall Jackson. Look, it got out of control. We were supposed to set up a perimeter, search for weapons, take one guy out in particular, this labor organizer, one object lesson, that's all, they used to call it a Christmas tree, a few ornaments hanging off the branches in the morning, you with me? But the guy runs inside the church and the priest starts yelling at our people out on the steps, and *pop pop pop,* what was I supposed to do, man? Suddenly I got a feeding frenzy on my hands.

You got to look at the overview to see my problem. It's in a cup of mountains, with nobody to see what's going on. That can be a big temptation. In the center of the ville is this stucco church with three little bell towers on it. The priest looks like a pool of black paint poured down the steps. The streets run off in all directions, like spokes on a wheel, and the guys who did the priest are scared and start popping anybody in sight. Before I know it, they're down all the spokes, deep in the ville, the circus tent's on fire, and I'm one fucking guy.

Geese and chickens are exploding out of the yards, pigs squealing, women screaming, people getting pulled into the street by their hair. She comes around a corner, like she's walking against a wind, and it takes everything in her to keep walking toward the sounds that make most people cover their ears and hide. I ain't ever going to forget the look in her face, she had these ice-blue eyes and hair like white corn silk and blood on her blouse, like it was thrown from an ink pen, but she saw it all, man, just like that whole street and the dead people in it zoomed right through her eyes onto a piece of film. The problem got made right there.

I pushed her hard. She had bones like a bird, you could hold her up against a candle and count them with your finger, I bet, and her face was a little pale triangle and I knew why she was a religious woman and I shoved her again. "This is an accident. It's ending now. You haul your butt out of here, Dutchie," I said.

I squeezed her arm, twisted her in the other direction,

scraped her against the wall, and saw the pain jump in her face. But they're hard to handle when they're light; they don't have any weight you can use against them. She pulled out of my hands, slipped past me, even cut me with her nails so she could keep looking at the things she wasn't supposed to see, that were going to mess all of us up. Her lips moved but I couldn't understand the words, the air between the buildings was sliced with muzzle flashes, like red scratches against the dark, and you could see empty shell casings shuddering across the lamplight in the windows. Then I heard the blades on the Huey before I felt the downdraft wash over us, and I watched it set down in a field at the end of this stone street and the two officers from the special school at Benning waiting for me, their cigars glowing inside the door, and I didn't have any doubt how it was going to go.

They said it in Spanish, then in English. Then in Spanish and English together. "It is sad, truly. But this one from Holland is *communista*. She is also very *serio,* with friends in the left-wing press. *Entiende, Señor Pogue?*"

It wasn't a new kind of gig. You throw a dozen bodies out at high altitudes. Sometimes they come right through a roof. Maybe it saves lives down the line. But she was alive when they brought her on board. Look, chief, I wasn't controlling any of it. My choices were I finish the mission, clean up these guys' shit, and not think about what's down below—because the sun was over the ridges now and you could see the tile roof of the church and the body of the labor organizer hanging against the wall and Indians running around like an ants' nest that's been stepped on—or stay behind and wait for some seriously pissed-off rebels to come back into the ville and see what we'd done.

Two guys tried to lift her up and throw her out, but she fought with them. So they started hitting her, both of them, then kicking her with their boots. I couldn't take it, man. It was like somebody opened a furnace door next to my head. This stuff had to end. She knew it, too, she saw it in my eyes even before I picked her up by her shoulders, almost like I was saving her, her hands resting on my cheeks, all the while staring into my eyes, even while I was carrying her to the door, even when she was framed against the sky, like she was inside a painting, her hair whipping in the wind, her face jerking back toward the valley floor and what was waiting for her, no stopping any of it now, chief, and I could see white lines in her scalp and taste the dryness and fear on her breath, but her lips were moving again while I squeezed her arms tighter and moved her farther out into a place where nobody had to make decisions anymore, her eyes like holes full of blue sky, and this time I didn't need to hear the words, I could read them on her mouth, they hung there in front of me even while the wind tore her out of my hands and she became just a speck racing toward the earth: You must change your way.

The Night
Johnny Ace Died

e and Big Mama Thornton were taking a break backstage when it happened. The dance floor was covered with Mexican and black people, a big haze of cigarette and reefer smoke floating over their heads in the spotlights. White people were up in the balcony, mostly low-rider badasses wearing pegged drapes and needle-nose stomps and girls who could do the dirty bop and manage to look bored while they put your flopper on autopilot. Then we heard it, one shot, *pow,* like a small firecracker. Johnny's dressing-room door was partly opened and I swear I saw blood fly across the wall, just before people started running in all directions.

Everyone said he had been showing off with a .22, spinning the cylinder, snapping the hammer on what should have been an empty chamber. But R&B and rock 'n' roll could be a dirty business back then, get my drift? Most of the musicians, white and black, were right out of the cotton field or the Assembly of God Church. The promoters and the record company executives were not. Guess whose names always ended up on the song credits, regardless of who wrote the song?

But no matter how you cut it, on Christmas night, 1954, Johnny Ace joined the Hallelujah Chorus and Eddy Ray Holland and I lost our chance to be the rockabillies who integrated R&B. Johnny had promised to let our band back him when he sang "Pledging My Love" that night. In those days Houston wasn't exactly on the cutting edge of the civil rights movement. We might have gotten lynched, but it would have been worth it. Listen to "Pledging My Love" sometime and tell me you wouldn't chuck your box in the suburbs and push your boss off a roof to be seventeen and hanging out at the drive-in again.

Nineteen fifty-four was the same year we met the kid from Mississippi Eddy Ray used to call the Greaser, because that boogie haircut of his looked like it had been hosed down with 3-in-One oil. But teenage girls went apeshit when the Greaser came onstage at the Louisiana Hayride, screaming their heads off, throwing their panties at him, crushing the roof of his Caddy to get into his hotel window, tearing out each other's hair over one of his socks. I even felt sorry for him. When they got finished with him, he usually looked like he'd been shot out of a cannon.

"I think the guy is a spastic. It's not an act," Eddy Ray said.

"Johnny Ray wears a hearing aid onstage. Fats Domino's mother probably thought she gave birth to a bowling ball," I said. "Jerry Lee looks like somebody slammed a door on his head. The Greaser played on Beale Street with Furry Lewis and Ike Turner. Give the guy some credit."

"Shut up, R.B.," Eddy Ray said.

I didn't argue. I knew Eddy Ray didn't carry grudges or envy people. Things just weren't going well for our band, that's all. The beer-joint circuit was full of guys like us, most of them talented and not in it for the money, either. On average the total pay wasn't more than fifty bucks a gig. The whole band usually traveled and slept in a couple of cars with the drums in the trunk and the other instruments roped on top. We lived on Vienna sausage, saltine crackers, and Royal Crown Colas, and brushed our teeth and took our baths in gas station lavatories.

The big difference with our group was Eddy Ray. He played boogie-woogie and blues piano and a Martin acoustic guitar and could make oil-field workers wipe their eyes when he sang "The Wild Side of Life."

Girls dug him, too. He had a profile like the statues of those Greek heroes, with the same kind of flat chest and stomach muscles that looked like rolls of quarters and

smooth skin that had never been tattooed. Not many people knew that Eddy Ray still heard bugles blowing in the
hills south of the Yalu River. I was at the Chosin Reservoir,
too, but Eddy Ray got grabbed and spent over two years at
a prisoner-of-war camp in a place called No Name Valley.
He always said four hundred of our soldiers got moved up
into Red China, where they were used in medical experi-
ments. I could tell when he was thinking about it because
the skin around his left eye would twitch like a bumblebee
was fixing to light on it.

So why would a stand-up guy like Eddy Ray be bothered by a kid from Tupelo, Mississippi?

Remember when I mentioned the gals who could start
your flopper flipping around in your slacks like it has a
brain of its own? This one's nickname was the Gin Fizz
Kitty from Texas City. She had gold hair, cherry lipstick,
and blue eyes that could look straight up into yours like you
were the only guy on the planet. When Eddy Ray and I
first saw her, six months before we were supposed to have
our breakthrough moment with Johnny Ace, she was
singing at a roadhouse called Buster's in Vinton, Louisiana.
Outside, the heat had started to go out of the day, and
through the screens we could see a lake and beyond it a red
sun shining through a grove of live oak trees. We were at
the bar, drinking long-necked Jax and eating crab burgers,
a big-bladed window fan blowing cool in our faces, but
Eddy Ray couldn't concentrate on the fine evening and the
good food and the coldness of the beer. His attention was
fixed on the girl at the microphone and the way her purple

cowboy shirt puffed and dented and changed colors in the breeze from the floor fan, the way she closed her eyes when she opened her mouth to sing, like she was offering up a prayer.

"What a voice. I'm going to ask her over," he said.

"I think I've seen her before, Eddy Ray," I said.

"Where?"

I looked at his expression, the sincerity in it, and wanted to kick myself. "At the Piggly Wiggly in Beaumont," I said.

"Thanks for passing that on, R.B."

He invited her to have a beer with us during her break. She didn't drink beer, she said. She drank gin fizzes. And she drank more of them in fifteen minutes than I ever saw anyone consume in my life. I thought we were going to get hit with a bar bill that would bankrupt us for the next month. But it all went on her tab, which told me she had a special relationship with the owner. When Eddy Ray went to the can, she smiled sweetly and asked, "You got some reason for staring at me, R.B.? I know you from somewhere?"

"No, ma'am, I don't think so," I replied, my face as blank as a shingle.

"If you got a haircut and tucked in your shirt and pulled up your britches, you'd be right handsome. But don't stare at people. It's impolite."

"I won't, I promise," I said, and wondered what we were fixing to get into.

I soon found out. Kitty Lamar Rochon's voice could

make the devil join the Baptist Church. When she and Eddy Ray did a number together, the dancers stopped and gathered around the bandstand as if angels had descended into their midst. It didn't take long for Eddy Ray to develop a very strong attraction for the Gin Fizz Kitty from Texas City. No, that doesn't describe it. It was more like he'd been run over by a train. So how do you tell your best friend he's been suckered and poleaxed by the town pump? Nope, "town pump" isn't the right term, either.

There was a chain of whorehouses that ran all the way along the Texas and Louisiana coast, all of them run by two Italian crime families that operated out of Galveston and New Orleans. How does a girl as pretty as Kitty Lamar end up in a cathouse? Believe it or not, most of the girls in those places were good-looking, some of them even beautiful. It was the times. Poor people didn't always have the choices they got today. Don't ask me how I know about this stuff, either.

So I didn't say diddly-squat to Eddy Ray. But, man, was it eating my lunch. For example, one week after Johnny Ace capped himself (or had somebody do it for him), we were blowing down the road in Eddy Ray's '49 Hudson, headed toward our next gig, a town up in Arkansas that was so small it was located between two Burma Shave signs. Kitty Lamar was lying down in the backseat, airing her bare feet, with the toenails painted red, out the window. She was popping bubble gum and reading a book on, get this, French existentialism, and commenting on it while she turned the pages. Then out of nowhere she lowered her book and said, "I wish you'd stop giving me them strange looks, R.B."

"*Excuse* me," I said.

"What's with you two?" Eddy Ray said, one hand on the wheel, a deck of Lucky Strikes wrapped in the sleeve of his T-shirt.

The previous night at the motel I'd heard her talking on the phone to the Greaser. It was obvious to me Kitty Lamar and the Greaser had known each other for some time and I'm talking about in the biblical sense. Eddy Ray had evidently decided to let bygones be bygones, but in my opinion she kept doing things that were highly suspicious. For example again, she loved fried oysters and catfish po'boy sandwiches. Then we'd be playing a gig around Memphis and she wouldn't touch a fish or shrimp or oyster dinner with a dung fork. Why is this significant? The Greaser was notorious for not allowing his punch of the day to eat anything that smelled of fish. Is that sick or what?

"Why don't we stop at that seafood joint up the road yonder and tank down a few deep-fried catfish sandwiches?" I said. "I know Kitty Lamar would dearly appreciate one."

She gave me a look that would scald the paint off a battleship.

"It doesn't matter to me one way or another, because I don't eat seafood this far inland," she said, her nose pointed in her book.

"Why is that, Kitty Lamar?" I asked, turning around in the seat, my face full of interest.

"Because that's how you get ptomaine poison. Most people who went past the eighth grade know that. Have you ever applied for a public library card, R.B.? When we get back to Houston, I'll show you how to fill out the form."

"Am I the only sane person in this car?" Eddy Ray said.

On Saturday night we played a ramshackle dance hall in the Arkansas Delta, just west of the Mississippi Bridge. Snow was blowing and Christmas lights were strung all over the outside of the building, so that the place glowed like a colored jewel inside the darkness. The tables and bar and dance floor were crowded with people who believed the live country music shows from Shreveport, Nashville, and Wheeling, West Virginia, represented a world of magic and celebrity and wealth that was hardly imaginable to them. Probably everybody in our band had grown up chopping cotton and picking ticks off themselves in a sluice of well water from a windmill pump, but onstage, here in the Delta, or a hundred places like it, we were sprinkled with stardust and maybe even immortality.

You know the secret to being a rockabilly or country music celebrity? It's not just the sequins on your clothes and the needle-nosed, mirror-shined boots. Your music has to be full of sorrow, I mean just like the blood-flecked, broken body of Jesus on the Cross. When people go to the Assembly of God Church and look up at that Cross, the pain they see there isn't in Jesus' body, it's in their own lives. I'm talking about droughts, dust storms, mine blowouts, black lung disease, or pulling cotton bolls or breaking corn till the tips of their fingers bleed. I went to school with kids who wore clothes sewn from Purina feed sacks. Eddy Ray was one of them. What I'm trying to say is we come from a class of people who think of misery as a given. They just want somebody who's had a degree of success to treat them with respect.

We'd all been in the dumps since Johnny died, me more than anybody, although I couldn't tell you exactly why. It was like our innocence had died with him. In fact, I felt sick thinking about it. I'd look over at the Gin Fizz Kitty from Texas City and hear that peckerwood accent, which sounded like somebody pulling a strand of baling wire through a tiny hole in a tin can, and I'd flat want to lie down on the highway and let a hog truck run over my head. A group of Yankees by the name of Bill Haley and the Comets were calling themselves the founders of rock 'n' roll and we were playing towns where families in need of excitement drove out on the highway to look at the new Coca-Cola billboard. And Johnny was dead, maybe not by his own hand, and his friends had gotten a whole lot of gone between him and them.

But that night in the Arkansas Delta, with the dancers shaking the whole building, it was like we were young again, unmarked by death, and the earth was green and so was the country and wonderful things were about to happen for all of us. We didn't take a break for two hours. When Eddy Ray ripped out Albert Ammons's "Swanee River Boogie" on the piano, the place went zonk. Then we kicked it up into E-major overdrive with Hank's "Lovesick Blues" and Red Foley's "Tennessee Saturday Night," Eddy

Ray and Kitty Lamar sharing the vocals. I got to admit it, the voices of those two could have started a new religion.

The snow stopped and a big brown moon came up over the hills, just as Guess Who walked in. You got it. The Greaser himself, along with Carl Perkins and Jerry Lee, all three of them decked out in sport coats, two-tone shoes, and slacks with knife-edged creases, their open-neck print shirts crisp and right out of the box. They sat at a front-row table and ordered long-neck beers and French-fried potatoes cooked in chicken fat. In less than two minutes half the women in the place were jiggling and turning around in their chairs like they'd just been fed horse laxative.

"What's he doing here?" Eddy Ray said.

Duh, I thought. But all I said was, "He's probably just tagging along with Jerry Lee and Carl. Sure is a nice night, isn't it?"

Then Kitty Lamar came back from the ladies' can and said, her eyes full of pure blue innocence, as though she had no idea the Greaser was going to be there: "Look, all the fellows from Sun Records are here. Are you gonna introduce them, Eddy Ray?"

Eddy Ray looked through the side window at the moon. The hills were sparkling with snow, the sky black and bursting with stars. "I haven't given real thought to it," he said. "Maybe you should introduce them, Kitty Lamar. Maybe you could sing a duet. Or maybe even do a three- or a four-some."

"How'd you like to get your face slapped?" she replied, chewing gum, rolling her eyes.

Eddy Ray pulled the mike loose from the stand, kicking a lot of dirty electronic feedback into the speaker system, like fingernails raking down a blackboard. His cheeks were flushed with color that had the irregular shape of fire, his eyes dark in a way I had not seen them before. He asked Carl and Jerry Lee and the Greaser to stand up, then he paused, as though he couldn't find the proper words to say. The whole joint was as quiet as a church house. I could feel sweat breaking on my forehead, because I knew the pain Eddy Ray was experiencing, and I knew the memories from the war that lived in his dreams, and I'd always believed part of him died in that prisoner-of-war camp south of the Yalu. I believed Eddy Ray carried a stone bruise in his heart, and if he felt he had been betrayed by the people he loved, he was capable of doing bad things, maybe not to others, but certainly to Eddy Ray. It wasn't coincidence that he and Johnny Ace had been pals.

The floor lights on the stage were wrapped with amber and yellow cellophane, but they seemed to burn red circles into my eyes. Jerry Lee and Carl were starting to look uncomfortable and the crowd was, too, like something really embarrassing was about to happen.

"Say something!" Kitty Lamar whispered.

But Eddy Ray just kept staring at the Greaser, like he was seeing his past or himself or maybe our whole generation before we went to war.

The Greaser glanced sideways, scratched at a place under one eye, then started to sit down.

"These guys are not only great musicians," Eddy Ray began, "they're three of the best guys I ever knew. It's an honor to have them here tonight. It's an honor to be their friend. They make me proud to be an American."

I thought the yelling and table-pounding from the crowd was going to blow the glass out of the windows.

The rest of the night should have been wonderful. It wasn't. Not for me, at least. In my lifetime I guess I've known every kind of person there is—brig rats, pimps, drug pushers, disk jockeys on the take, promoters who split for Vegas with the cashbox, and, my favorite bunch, scrubbed-down ministers who preach Jesus on Sunday and Wednes-day night and the rest of the week screw teenage girls in their congregations. But none of them can hold a candle to a friend who stabs you in the back. That kind of person not only steals your faith in your fellow human beings, he makes you resent yourself.

We had taken a break about 11:30 p.m., figuring to do one more set before we called it a night, and I hadn't seen the Greaser in the last hour or so. I glanced out the back window at a gazebo that was perched up on a little hill above a picnic area. I couldn't believe what I saw.

Silhouetted against the moon, the Greaser and Kitty Lamar were both standing inside the gazebo, the Greaser bending down toward her so their foreheads were almost touching, her ta-tas standing up inside her cowboy shirt like the upturned noses on a pair of puppy dogs. I felt sick in-side. No, that doesn't describe it. I wanted to tear the

Greaser apart and personally drive Kitty Lamar down to the bus depot and throw her and her puppy dogs on the first westbound headed for Big D and all points south.

But that would have been easy compared to what I knew I had to do. I'd kept my silence ever since we'd first met Kitty Lamar at the roadhouse in Vinton. Now I was the guy who'd have to drive the nail through Eddy Ray's heart. Or at least that was what I told myself.

I waited until he and I were alone, at breakfast, the next day, in a restaurant with big windows that looked out on the Mississippi River. Eddy Ray was fanging down a plate of fried eggs, ham, grits, and toast and jam, hammering ketchup all over it, his face rested and happy.

"I got to tell you something," I said.

"It's not necessary. Eat up."

"You don't even know what I was gonna say."

"You're worried about the Greaser. I had a talk with him last night. Kitty Lamar and him are just friends."

"Yeah?" I said.

"You got a hearing problem?"

I stared out the window at a tug pushing a long barge piled with shale. The barge had gotten loose and was scraping against the pilings of the bridge. The port side had tipped upward against a piling and gray mounds of shale were sliding through the starboard deck rail, sinking as rapidly as concrete in the current.

"I saw her about five years back in a Port Arthur cathouse," I said.

Eddy Ray studied the barge out on the river, chewing his food, his hair freshly barbered, razor-edged on the neck. "What were you doing there?"

"I got a few character defects myself. Least I don't go around claiming to be something I'm not," I said.

"Kitty Lamar already told me about it. So quit fretting your mind and your bowels over other people's business. I swear, R.B., I think you own stock in an aspirin company."

"I've heard her talking to him on the phone, Eddy Ray. They're taking you over the hurdles. I saw them in the gazebo last night, too. They looked like Siamese twins joined at the forehead."

This time he couldn't slip the punch and I saw the light go out of his eyes. He cut a small piece of ham and put it in his mouth. "I guess that puts a different twist on it," he said.

I hated myself for what I had just done.

Could it get worse? When we got back to the motel, the desk clerk told Eddy Ray to call the long-distance operator.

"Nobody answered the phone in my room?" Eddy Ray said.

"No, sir," the clerk said.

Kitty Lamar was supposed to have met us in the diner but hadn't shown up. Evidently she hadn't hung around the room, either. Eddy Ray got the callback operator on the line and she connected him with our agent in Houston, a guy who for biblical example had probably modeled his life on Pontius Pilate's.

The agency had booked us in a half-dozen places in Tennessee, Mississippi, and Louisiana, but as of that morning all our dates were canceled.

"What gives, Leon?" Eddy Ray said into the receiver. He was standing by the bed, puffing on a Lucky Strike while he listened, his back curved like a question mark. "Investigation? Into what? Listen to me, Leon, we didn't see anything, we don't know anything, we didn't do anything. I've got a total of thirty-seven dollars and forty cents to get us back to Houston. The air is showing through my tires. Are you listen—"

The line went dead. Eddy Ray removed the receiver from his ear, stared at it, and replaced it in the telephone cradle. "Do you have to be bald-headed to get a Fuller Brush route?" he said.

"Leon sold us out for another band?" I said.

"He says some Houston cops want to question us about Johnny's death."

"Why us?"

"They wonder if we saw a certain guy in Johnny's dressing room." Then Eddy Ray mentioned the name of a notorious promoter in the music business, a Mobbed-up guy who operated on both sides of the color line and scared both black and white people cross-eyed.

I felt my mouth go dry, my stomach constrict, the kind of feeling I used to get when I'd hear the first sounds of small-arms fire, like strings of Chinese firecrackers popping.

"We'll go to California. You know what they say, 'Nobody dies in Santa Barbara.' How far is Needles from Santa Barbara?"

But it wasn't funny. We'd had it and we both knew it.

≋

The music business was corrupt back then. Disk jockeys took payola and people who got to the top were either humps for the Mafia or signed deals that left them with chump change. A black guy in Jennings, Louisiana, put out an R&B record that sold a million copies and netted him twenty-five dollars. Even the Greaser paid his manager fifty-one percent of his earnings.

When you got in trouble with the wrong people, you took up bottleneck guitar on a street corner or punched out your eyes and joined the Five Blind Boys. In our case, the wrong people was Cool Daddy Hopkins, a six-foot-six mulatto who wore three-piece suits, a yellow fedora, and popped matches on his thumbnail to light his Picayune cigarettes. He not only carried a nickel-plated, pearl-handled derringer, he shot and killed a white man in Mississippi with it and wasn't lynched or even prosecuted.

Northerners always thought the South was segregated. Wrong. Money was money, sex was sex, music was music, and color didn't have squat to do with any of it. Some people said Johnny Ace might have gotten in Cool Daddy's face one too many times. I didn't know if that was true or not. But when we got back from our gig in Arkansas, the

Houston cops questioned us about Johnny and his relationship with Cool Daddy. Our names ended up on the front page of two Houston newspapers. In the world of R&B and rockabilly music, we had become the certifiable stink on shit.

Kitty Lamar and Eddy Ray had called it quits, even though you could tell neither one wanted to let go of the other. I wanted to blame the Greaser for busting them up, but I couldn't forget the fact it was me who told Eddy Ray that Kitty Lamar was probably bumping uglies behind his back.

That's what I did for the guy who had carried me three hundred yards across a corrugated rice paddy while bullets from Chinese burp guns popped snow around his bootlaces.

We played at a carnival up in Conroe and at a dance in Bandera and didn't clear enough to cover gas and hamburgers and the tire we blew out on a cattle guard. The boys in the band started to drift off, one by one, and join other groups. I couldn't blame them. We'd been jinxed six ways from breakfast ever since Johnny had died. Finally, Eddy Ray and I admitted defeat ourselves and got jobs as roughnecks on a drilling rig outside Galveston.

He wrote one song he called "The Oil Driller's Lament." We recorded it on a 45 rpm that cost us four dollars in a recording booth on the old Galveston amusement pier, with Eddy Ray singing and me backing him up on harmonica and Dobro. This is how it went:

Ten days on, five days off,
I guess my blood is crude oil now,
Don't give your heart to a gin-fizz kitty
From the back streets of Texas City,
'Cause you won't ever lose
Them mean ole roughnecking blues.

It was a song about faded love and betrayal and honky-tonk angels and rolling down lost highways that led to jail, despair, and death. Some of the lyrics in it even scared me. It was sunset when we made the recording, and the sky was green, the breakers sliding through the pilings under the pier, the air smelling of salt and fried shrimp and raindrops that made rings in the swells. A lot of country singers fake the sadness in their songs, but when Eddy Ray sang this one, it was real and it broke my heart.

"What you studying on?" he asked.

"I messed you up with Kitty Lamar," I said.

He spun our four-dollar recording on his index finger, his face handsome and composed in the wind off the Gulf. "Kitty Lamar loved another guy. It ain't her fault. That's the way love is. It picks you, you don't pick it," he said.

The sun was the dull red color of heated iron when it first comes out of the forge. I could feel the pier creak with the incoming tide and smell the salty bitterness of dried fish blood in the boards. I watched the sun setting on the horizon and the thunderheads gathering in the south, and I felt like the era we lived in and had always taken for granted was ending, but I couldn't explain why.

"Hey, you and me whipped the Chinese army, R.B. They just haven't figured that out yet," he said. "There's worse things than being an oil-drilling man. I'm extremely copacetic on this."

≋

I mentioned to you that we were jinxed six ways from breakfast? The next morning, with no blowout preventer on the wellhead, our drill bit punched into a pay sand at a depth where nobody expected to find oil. The pipe geysered out of the hole under thousands of pounds of pressure, clanging like a freight train through the superstructure. Then a spark jumped off a steel surface, and a torrent of flaming gas and oil ballooned through the derrick and melted the whole rig as though the spars were made of licorice.

Eddy Ray and I sat on the deck of a rescue boat, our hair singed, our clothes peppered with burn holes, and watched the fire boil under the water.

"Does Cool Daddy Hopkins still have his office in the Fifth Ward?" he said.

≋

Houston's black district was its own universe. It was even patrolled by black cops, although the department gave them only dilapidated squad cars, usually with big dents in them, to drive around in. There were bars and barbecue joints and shoeshine stands on almost every street corner. You could hear music from radios, jukeboxes, church houses, old black guys jamming under an oak tree. Dig this. In the black district there were no record stores. Both 78 and 45 rpm records were always sold at beauty and barbershops. The owners hung loudspeakers outside their business to advertise whatever new records had just come in, so all day long the street was filled with the sounds of Gatemouth Brown, Laverne Baker, and the Platters.

Cool Daddy Hopkins had his office in the back of a barbershop, where he sat in front of a big fan, a chili dog covered with melted cheese and a bottle of Mexican beer on his desk. Cool Daddy had gold skin with moles on it that looked like drops of mud that had been splashed on him from a passing car. His coat and vest hung on the back of a chair, along with a .32 derringer stuffed in a shoulder holster. His silk shirt was the color of tin, pools of sweat looped under his pits.

He kept eating, sipping from his beer, his eyes never blinking while he listened to what Eddy Ray had to say. "So you think I'm the guy keeping you off the circuit?" he said.

"I'm not here to make accusations. I'm just laying it out for you, Cool Daddy. Johnny was my friend, but I don't know what happened in that dressing room," Eddy Ray said. "We told the cops that. Now we're telling you. We're eighty-sixed and shit-canned all over the South."

"Sorry to hear that. But life's a bitch, then you die, right?" Cool Daddy said. He reached into a cooler by his foot and slipped a beer out of ice that had been pounded and crushed in a cloth bag with a rolling pin. He made a ring with his thumb and index finger and wiped the ice off the bottle onto the floor. There were a couple of glasses turned top-down on a shelf above his head. I thought he was going to offer us a beer to split. Instead, he cracked off the cap with a bottle opener and drank from the neck.

"Johnny and me was both in the United States Navy, ammunition loaders, can you dig that?" he said. "You know who was loading right next to me? Harry Belafonte. That's no jive, man."

But Eddy Ray wasn't listening. "Our agent says he doesn't want trouble with you. So if you're not the problem, why is Leon telling us that?" Eddy Ray said.

The sunlight through the window seemed to grow warmer, more harsh, in spite of the fan, the air suddenly close and full of dust particles and the smell of hair tonic from the shop up front. " 'Cause Leon is like most crackers. If he ain't got a colored man to blame for his grief, he got to look in the mirror and put it on his own sorry-ass self."

Eddy Ray leaned forward in his chair and stuck an unlit Lucky Strike in his mouth, fishing in his jeans for a match. His hair was uncut, wet and combed straight back, curly on the back of his neck. "Give us another R&B gig."

"The train went through the station and you ain't caught it, man. Wish it'd been different, but it ain't," Cool Daddy said.

Eddy Ray found a book of matches but lost his concentration and put them away. He took the Lucky Strike out of his mouth and brushed at his nose with the back of his wrist. "I'll put it another way. If you cain't see your way to hep us, just stay the hell out of our sandbox," he said.

"You still don't get it, do you?" Cool Daddy replied, a smile tugging at the corner of his mouth.

"Get what?"

"I ain't the power in this game. Who you think screwed you on the circuit, boy? Who got that kind of power?"

Eddy Ray's eyes blinked, but not in time to hide the glow of recognition in them.

"Yeah, that's right," Cool Daddy said. "The word is your lady friend been bad-mouthing you with certain people at Sun Record Company. The word is they don't like you, motherfucker, particularly a certain boy from Mis-'sippi don't like you."

Cool Daddy pinched his temples, like he was struggling not to hurt the feelings of dumb white people such as ourselves. "Let me strap it on you, boy. I thought maybe she was leaking info about me to the cops, so I had a detective get ahold of her phone records." Then he mentioned the name of a powerful man he said Kitty Lamar had phoned repeatedly at Sun Records. "I don't know what you done to her, but I think she fixed yo' ass good."

The only sound in the room was the vibration of the electric fan. Eddy Ray's eyes looked like brown pools that someone had filled with black silt.

"He was lying," I said when we were outside.

"You're the one who told me Kitty Lamar was a Judas. You cain't have it both ways, R.B."

"I'm going out west," I said.

We were in traffic, headed toward Eddy Ray's house in the Heights section of North Houston, oak trees sweeping by us on wide boulevards, where termite-eaten nineteenth-century houses with wide galleries sat gray and hot-looking in the shade. I couldn't believe what I'd just said and the implication it had for my friendship with Eddy Ray. He finally lit the cigarette he'd been fiddling with since Cool Daddy's office.

"Am I invited?" he asked.

"Nobody can help you, Eddy Ray. You don't think you should have survived the war and I think you're aiming to take both of us down."

"Sorry to hear you say that." He flipped the dead paper match into the traffic.

I got out of the Hudson at the red light and went into the first bar I could find. Lone Star and Jax beer might seem like poor solace for busted careers and lost friendships, but I figured if I drank enough of it, it would have to count for something. And that's exactly what I did, full-tilt, for the next six months.

≈≈≈

I also spent some time in the Houston City Jail for my third arrest as a public drunk. I picked watermelons in the Rio

Grande Valley and rode a freight train west and cut lettuce in El Centro. I played Dobro for tips in bars on East Fifth Street in Los Angeles, followed the wheat harvest all the way to Saskatoon, and ended up on Larimer Street in Denver, where I met Cisco Houston and played as a guest on his syndicated radio show, right before he got blacklisted.

I saw the country from the bottom side up. I may have married a three-hundred-pound Indian woman on the Southern Ute Reservation, but I can't be sure, because by the time I sobered up from all the peyote buttons I'd eaten, I was in an uncoupled boxcar full of terrified illegal farmworkers, roaring at eighty miles an hour down Raton Pass into New Mexico. And that's what led to me to one of those moments in life when you finally figure out there are no answers to the big mysteries, like why the innocent suffer, why there's disease and war, and all that kind of stuff. I also figured out that what we call our destiny is usually determined by two or three casual decisions which on the surface seem about as important as spitting your gum through a sewer grate.

The sky was still black and sprinkled with stars when I crawled off the boxcar at the bottom of the grade in Raton. Then the sun broke above the crest of the hills and the entire countryside looked soaked in blood, the arroyos deep in shadow, the cones of dead volcanoes stark and biscuit-colored against the sky. I could smell pinion trees, wet sage, woodsmoke, cattle in the pastures, and creek water that had melted from snow. I could smell the way the country probably was when it was only a dream in the mind of God.

I found a bar by the railway tracks but didn't go in. Instead, I walked down to a café built out of stucco, networked with heat cracks, where a bunch of Mexican gandy walkers were eating breakfast. I had one dollar and seven cents in my pocket, enough to order scrambled eggs, a pork sausage patty, fried spuds, and coffee, and to leave a dime tip.

While I sipped coffee, I thumbed through a three-day-old copy of an Albuquerque newspaper. On an inside page was a story about none other than the Greaser. I had read enough stories about the Greaser's career to last me a lifetime, but in the third paragraph was a statement that was like a thumbtack in the eye. According to the reporter, the Greaser had left Sun Records at least a year ago and had signed a managerial deal with a guy who used to be a carnival barker.

"You okay, hon?" the waitress said to me. She was a big redheaded woman with upper arms like cured hams, and perfume you could probably smell all the way to Flagstaff.

"Me? I'm fine. Except for the fact I'm probably the dumbest sonofabitch who ever walked into your café," I said.

"No, that was my ex-husband. There's some showers for truck drivers in back. It's on the house," she said. She winked at me. "Hang around, cowboy."

Life on the underside of America could have its moments.

Five days later, I climbed down from the cab of a

tractor-trailer and walked four blocks through a run-down, tree-shaded neighborhood to Eddy Ray's house. He had scraped up a pile of black leaves and moldy pecan husks in his side yard and was burning them in an oil can, his eyes watering in the smoke.

I dropped my duffel bag on the gallery and sat down in the glider and waited for him to say hello.

"It's me, in case you haven't noticed the man sitting about ten feet to your rear," I said.

"I got your postcard from the Big Horn County Jail," he said, fanning smoke out of his face.

I didn't remember writing a card from jail, but that wasn't unusual considering the number of organic chemical additives I had been putting into my brain. "Remember when I told you Cool Daddy Hopkins was lying about Kitty Lamar?"

"I do."

"Know why you wouldn't believe me?" I said.

"Not interested."

" 'Cause Cool Daddy fooled me, too. I thought Kitty Lamar had stuck it to us. Know why I thought that?"

He leaned on a rake handle, shutting his eyes, maybe hoping I'd be gone when he opened them again.

" 'Cause I had a grudge against her from the first time we heard her sing," I said, answering my own question. " 'Cause I didn't want her coming between us."

I felt a little funny saying that and I let my eyes slip off his face. He picked up a huge sheaf of compacted leaves and dropped them into the flames. Thick curds of yellow smoke curled into the tree limbs overhead. "So what's changed?"

"When Cool Daddy told us Kitty Lamar had been bad-mouthing us at Sun Records, the Greaser had already been gone from Sun. Kitty Lamar didn't know anybody at Sun. The only person she knew there was the Greaser. Besides, why would people at the record company want to hurt us? Sun doesn't do business like that."

"You're sure about this?"

"I read it in the newspaper. Then I called the reference lady at the public library to check it out. The Greaser has been managed by this carnival barker or freak show manager or whatever he is for the last year."

Eddy Ray sat down on the steps, his back to me. His face and arms were bladed with the sunlight shining through the trees. He rubbed the back of his neck, like a terrible memory was eating its way through his skull.

"What's wrong?" I said.

"The Greaser called up and asked me to send him a demo. He said he'd take it to a studio for us. He said he'd always thought my voice was as good as Johnny Ace's."

"What'd you do?" I said.

"Told him he was a hypocrite and a liar and to lose my phone number."

At least I wasn't the only one in the band with a serious thinking disorder.

"Seen Kitty Lamar?" I said.

"I heard she was singing in a lounge in Victoria."

I pushed the glider back and forth, the chains creaking,

the worn-out heels of my cowboy boots dragging on the boards.

"I'm not gonna do it," he said, looking straight ahead at the yard.

"Do what?"

"What you're thinking. She can ring or come by if she wants to, but I ain't running after her. Will you stop playing on that glider? You're giving me a migraine."

"You got that 45 rpm we recorded on the amusement pier in Galveston?"

"What about it?"

"I paid half of the four dollars it cost to make it. I want to take my half to Victoria and let Kitty Lamar hear it. Then I'm going to send my half to the Greaser."

I said that to piss him off good, which sometimes was the only way you got Eddy Ray outside of his own head. He went inside the house and came back out with the 45. It was wrapped in soft tissue and taped around the edges, and I knew that Eddy Ray hadn't given up his music.

"Does Kitty Lamar still paint her toenails?" I asked.

"Why?"

" 'Cause I always thought they were real cute."

He stared at me as though he'd never seen me before.

And that's how our band came back together and that's how "The Oil Driller's Lament" went on the charts and stayed there for sixteen weeks. But Eddy Ray Holland and the Gin Fizz Kitty from Texas City were never an item again. That's because she married R. B. Benoit, Dobro player extraordinaire, also known as myself, in a little Assembly of God church in Del Rio, Texas. The church was right across the river from the Mexican radio station where, on a clear night, the Carter Family and Wolfman Jack beamed their radio shows high above the wheat fields and the mountains, all the way to the Canadian line, like a rainbow that has nowhere else to go.

Water

People

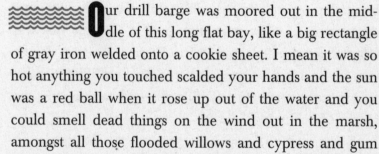 Our drill barge was moored out in the middle of this long flat bay, like a big rectangle of gray iron welded onto a cookie sheet. I mean it was so hot anything you touched scalded your hands and the sun was a red ball when it rose up out of the water and you could smell dead things on the wind out in the marsh, amongst all those flooded willows and cypress and gum trees. That was right before Hurricane Audrey hit the Louisiana coast in 1957. The thundershowers we got in the afternoon weren't anything more than hot steam, and when lightning hit on the sandbars, you could see it danc-

ing under the chop, flickering, like yellow snakes flipping
around in a barrel full of dark water.

Skeeter was our shooter, or dynamite man, and was
about forty years old and thought to be weird by everybody
on board, partly because he was a preacher over in Wiggins, Mississippi, but also because he had a way of coming
up behind you and running his hands down your hips. In
other words, he wasn't apt to make a skivvy run to Morgan
City, although that could have been because he was a religious man. The truth is doodlebuggers did the dirtiest work
in the oil field and it was no accident other people referred
to us as white niggers.

I watched Bobby Joe, our driller, drop the last six-can
stick of explosives down the pipe and feed the cap wire off
his palms. Bobby Joe's chest looked like it was carved from
a tree stump; it was lean and hard and tapered, swollen
with muscle under the arms, tanned the gold-brown color
of worn saddle leather. He had a BCD from the Crotch for
busting up a couple of S.P.'s. He told me once his little boy
drowned in a public swimming pool in Chicago that was
full of colored people and Puerto Ricans. The next day he
told me he'd lied because he was drunk and I'd better not
tell anybody what he'd said. Like I'm on board to write the
history of Bobby Joe Guidry.

I wrapped the cap wire around the terminals on
Skeeter's detonator and screwed down the wing nuts and
said, "You're lit, pappy," and everybody went aft or got on
the jugboat that was tied to the stern, and when Skeeter
gave it the juice, those eighteen cans of hot stuff went off

with a big *thrummmmmp* deep down in the earth and fish jumped all over the bay like they'd been shocked with an electric current. The force of the explosion kicked the drill barge's bow up in the air and slapped it back against the surface, then a second later brown water and sand and cap wire came geysering out of the pipe the way wildcat wells used to come in years ago, and a yellow cloud of smoke drifted back across the jugboat and filled the inside of your head with a smell like a freshly tarred gravel road.

Skeeter wore a long-sleeve denim shirt and a cork sun helmet and steel-rim glasses that caused him to crinkle his nose all the time. His face was round as a muskmelon, puffy with the humidity, always pink with fresh sunburn, and his eyes blue and watery and red along the rims, like they were irritated from the smoke that seeped out of the water after he'd zapped the juice into the hole and given things down below a real headache. Bobby Joe was wiping the drilling mud off his chest with a nasty towel he'd gotten out of the engine room. His hair was the color of dry straw under his tin hat and there was a green and red Marine Corps tattoo on his upper arm that was slick and bright with sweat.

"Y'all put too many cans down, Bobby Joe," Skeeter said.

Bobby Joe went on wiping at his hands with that rag and didn't even look up. "I tell you how to do your job, Skeet?" he said.

"We're killing fish we ain't got to. You can blow the casing out the hole, too," Skeeter said.

"You study on things too much." Bobby Joe still hadn't

looked up, he just kept on wiping at those big, flat hands of his that had scars like white worms on the backs of his fingers.

"Hit don't say nowhere we got to blow half the damn bay into the next parish," Skeeter said.

"Skeet, you put me in mind of an egg-sucking dog sniffing around a brooder house," Bobby Joe said. "I declare if you don't."

We knew it was a matter of time before one of those two ran the other off. The party chief would abide any kind of behavior that didn't hurt the job; that's why he'd let a liberty boat head for the hot-pillow joints in Morgan City the fifth night out on the hitch, about the time some guys would start messing around in the shower and pretend it was just grab-assing. But he wouldn't put up with guys hiding vodka in their seabags or fighting over cards or carrying a personal grief out on the drill barge, it got people hurt or killed, like the time this Mexican boy I'm fixing to tell you about fell off the bow and got sucked under the barge just when the skipper kicked over the screws, and not to be overlooked it cost the company a shitload of money.

His nickname was Magpie because he was missing two teeth up front and he had black hair with a patch like white paint in it. He weighed about three hundred pounds and traveled around the country eating lightbulbs and blowing fire in a carnival act when he wasn't doodlebugging. Bobby Joe said he saw him cheating in the bouree game and told him to his face. Magpie might have looked like a pile of whale shit but I saw him pick up a six-foot gator by its tail once, whip it around in the air, and heave it plumb across the barge's deck and leave two or three drillers with wee-wee in their socks. Magpie told Bobby Joe they were going to have a beer and learn some helpful hints about behavior when they got off the hitch, and Bobby Joe replied he knew just the spot because the dispenser for toilet seat covers in the can had a sign on it that said PEPPERBELLY PLACE MATS.

A week later we were way down at the mouth of the Atchafalaya, with storm winds capping the surface, and Magpie fell off the drill into the current and was swept down under the hull just as I was running at the bridge, waving my arms and yelling at the skipper, who was looking back over his shoulder at the jugboat with a cigarette in his mouth. This retarded kid on the jugboat was the first to see Magpie surface downstream. He vomited over the rail, then started screaming and running up and down on the deck till his father put him in the pilothouse and wiped his face and held his head against his chest. Think of water that runs by the discharge chute on a slaughterhouse. The thunder and wind were shrieking like the sky was being ripped loose from the earth. I don't care to revisit moments like that.

The quarterboat was moored with ropes to a willow island and at sunset Skeeter would stand out on the bow in the mosquitoes by himself, where all the sacks of drilling mud were stacked, or sometimes get in a pirogue and paddle back through the flooded trees. I used to think he was running a trotline but I found out different when he didn't think anybody was watching him. He had a paper bag full of these little plastic statues of Jesus, the kind people put on their dashboard, and he'd tie fish twine around the feet with a machinist's bolt on the other end and hold it to his head with his eyes squinted shut, then sink it in the water and paddle on to the next spot.

"You been out here long, W.J.?" he said when he was tying the pirogue back up.

"Not really."

I felt sorry for him; it wasn't right the way some guys made fun of him behind his back. He was at Saipan during the war. That was a lot more than most of us had done.

"You got something fretting you, Skeet?"

"A Mexican boy gets shredded up in the propeller and don't nobody seem bothered."

"Bobby Joe says Magpie was fooling around and hanging off the rail taking a whiz. It's just one of them things."

"Nobody else seen hit."

"Them ain't good thoughts, Skeet."

"Bobby Joe wasn't watching his little boy when he drowned in that swimming pool. He blames them other people for not saving him. I was in that bouree game. That Mexican boy wasn't cheating."

At breakfast on the quarterboat we got anything we wanted; you just had to pass through the galley and tell the cook: pancakes, eggs, stacks of bacon and fried ham, grits, coffee, cereal, white bread and butter and jam. Dinner was even better: steaks, fried chicken, meat loaf, gumbo and catfish on Fridays, mashed potatoes, rice and milk gravy, sweating pitchers of Kool-Aid and iced tea, cake or ice cream for dessert.

Lunchtimes, though, we were out on the drill barge and usually cooked up something pretty putrid, like Viennas and rice, in the small galley behind the bridge and ate it in the lee of the pilothouse. The sky was the color of scorched brass when Bobby Joe sniffed at the air and said to Skeeter, "Is there something dead out where you keep your dynamite at?"

"Could be," Skeeter said.

"It's mighty strong. You ought to do something about it, Skeet, wash it off in the shallows, slap some deodorant on it."

"I might have hit on my clothes. I ain't got hit on my conscience."

Bobby Joe puffed on a filter-tipped cigar without missing a beat. "I wish I was smart," he said. He leaned forward and tipped ashes off the side of the deck. "Then I could figure out how come I like girls and I didn't turn out to be a faggot. I'm here to tell you, boys, it's a pure mystery."

Skeeter stared at Bobby Joe and rolled a wood match back and forth across his false teeth. You could flat hear that match clicking it was so quiet.

〜〜〜

At quitting time that day, the party chief said anybody who wanted could go into the levee on the crewboat as long as they were back in the galley sober at 0600 the next morning. The upper deck of the quarterboat was divided into two rows of tiny one-man cabins, with the showers and a can at one end of the gangway and a recreation room with a big window fan, where we played cards, at the other. The rain had just stopped and the air was cool and smelled like fish and wet trees, with yellow and purple clouds piled out on the Gulf, wind blowing through the willow islands and mullet jumping where the sunlight still shone above the dead cypress; everybody was in a good mood, whistling, combing their hair with Lucky Tiger and butch wax, putting on starched khakis, skintight jeans, snap-button shirts, and hand-tooled belts with chrome buckles as big as Cadillac bumpers and Indian stitching along the edges.

Bobby Joe was sitting on the edge of his bunk, buffing the points of his black cowboy boots till the leather was full of little lights. Skeeter leaned against the hatchway with his arms folded across his chest, crinkling his nose under his glasses.

"What you want, Skeeter?"

"You ain't got to carry hit."

"Carry what? What the fuck are you talking about?"

"What happened to your little boy."

"I hate guys like you. You're always feeding off somebody's grief. You quit pestering me."

"I don't mean you no harm."

You could hear Bobby Joe breathing. Another guy had

just cut his hair for him out on deck, and there was a white stretch of skin half-mooned under the hairline on his neck. His hands opened and closed into rocks, his knuckles swelling up the size of quarters. Then he just about knocked Skeeter down tearing out the door into Skeeter's cabin.

He ripped the mattress back off Skeeter's bunk and grabbed the paper bag with all the little statues of Jesus in it, wadded it up in his hands, and pushed the screen out on the stick and flung the bag straight out into the willow and cypress trees. You could see it spinning in an eddy just before the paper turned dark with water and went under.

"Now you leave me alone," Bobby Joe said, his hands trembling at his sides, the veins in his forearms purple and thick as soda straws.

"All right, Bobby Joe. I promise I won't bother you no more," Skeeter said.

He wasn't expecting that.

I'd been to Claudette's before and always thought the girls were pretty nice, no worse or better than us, anyway, people don't always get to choose what they are, that's the way I figured it. Most of them came from mill or farm towns in Texas and Louisiana and Mississippi, the kind of towns where people worked in ammunition or roach-paste factories, places where hanging out at the Dairy Queen or down at the filling station was the biggest thing going on Saturday night, which wasn't the reason they got in the life, I think,

although that's what they tried to tell you when you asked
how they ended up in a hundred-year-old two-story house
next to colored town with a blue light over the door and the
paint eaten off the wood by the salt and a pimp in the front
room who once knocked the glass eye out of a girl for sass-
ing him.

You want to get one of them mad? Ask her about her father, what kind of guy was he, did he ever take her to a
kid's show or a county fair, did he know what happened to
her, did he care what happened to her, something like that,
and tell me about it. I never thought they were bad girls,
though. As long as you bought a beer, it was six bits for a
little-bitty Schlitz, you could talk to them, or listen to the
jukebox, and you didn't have to take one of them upstairs,
nobody'd bother you, really.

But I saw something that changed my thinking. It was a
weekday afternoon and business was slow except for a
roughneck who'd just been paid off his rig and three kids
with boogies, flattops with ducktails on the sides, and black
jeans and boots with steel taps and chains dripping off the
leather, the kind of stomp-ass stuff juvenile delinquents
wore back in those days. The roughneck was juiced to the
eyes, by himself, no crew to take care of him, and kept
splitting open his billfold and showing off his money to the
girls, like this would have them lining up to glom his
twanger.

One of the three kids said something about rolling the
guy. Then a girl pulled the kid over by the jukebox, you
could see them wreathed in cigarette smoke against the or-

ange and purple light from the plastic casing, their heads bent together like two question marks, her hair like white gold, her mouth glossy and red, she was pretty enough to make you hurt. I'll never forget what she said to him, because it wasn't just the words, it was the smile on the kid's face when she said it, like a twisted slit across bread dough, "Y'all take him somewhere else and do it, okay? Then come back and spend the money here."

It was pretty depressing.

After most of the others took off for the levee, I went out on the jugboat with Skeeter to move his dynamite caps and primers to a new sandbar. The caps and primers were a lot more sensitive than the actual dynamite, and he kept them in a big steel lockbox on a sandbar and he had to move the box every week or so to keep up with the drill barge.

"I wouldn't let it bother me, Skeet," I said. "Bobby Joe's got a two-by-four up his cheeks sometimes."

"Hit ain't him."

"So what's got you down?"

"My ministry ain't gone nowhere. Same back in Wiggins. I might as well be out talking in a vacant lot."

We unloaded the box, then heaved it empty up on the deck. The water was capping in the south and you could smell salt in the wind and see birds flying everywhere.

"Maybe if you went about it a little different," I said. "Sinking those little dashboard statues is a mite unusual."

"I done something I never could make up for," he said. "A bunch of Japs was down in a cave, maybe seventy or eighty of them. I blew the mountain in on top of them. You could hear a hum through the coral at night, like thousands of bees singing. It was all them men moaning down there."

He scratched a mosquito bite on his face and looked at the willow islands and the leaves that were starting to shred in the wind.

"Sometimes people have to do bad things in a war," I said.

"I almost had myself convinced they wasn't human. Then I seen them people going off the cliffs at Saipan. Women threw their babies first, then jumped after them, right on top of the rocks, they was so scared of us."

I pulled the anchor and we drifted out into the current. The sun's afterglow made a dark red light in the water.

"What's that got to do with statues?" I said.

"I bring Jesus to them people who jumped into the sea. The same water is wrapped all the way around the earth, ain't hit? Hit ain't that way with land. You could drive this boat from here to Saipan if you had a mind."

"I say don't grieve on it. I say let the church roll on, Skeeter."

But there was no consoling him. He sat on the deck rail, his face like an empty pie plate, and I kicked the engines over and hit it hard across the bay. The sky in the south had gone white as bone, the way it does when the barometer drops and no birds or other living things want to be out there.

Hurricane Audrey flat tore South Louisiana up. It killed maybe five hundred people in Cameron Parish, just south of Lake Charles, and left drowned people hanging in trees out in the marsh. We rode it out, though, with the wind screaming outside, houseboats spinning around upside down in the current, and coons climbing up the mooring ropes to hide from the rain on the lee side of the deck.

Then the third day the sun rose up out of the steam like a yellow balloon over the cypress trees and we were climbing back on the crewboat and headed for the drill barge again. The night before, I'd been out looking for a bunch of recording jugs that got washed overboard, and till we picked up the dynamite caps and primers at the lockbox out on the sandbar, I didn't even notice Skeeter was gone and we had a new shooter on board, a man with a steel-gray military haircut and skin the color of chewing tobacco who didn't have much to say to anybody and worked a crossword puzzle. Everybody was enjoying the ride out to the barge, smoking hand-rolls, drinking coffee, relaxing on the cushions while the bow slapped across the waves and the spray blew back over the windows, when I asked, "Where's Skeeter at?"

Suddenly nobody had diddly-squat on a rock to say.

"Where's he at?" I said.

"He drug up last night," one fellow finally said.

"That don't make sense. He would have told me," I said.

"He got run off, W.J.," another guy said.

"The hell he was," I said. Then I said it again, "The hell he was."

All I could see were the backs of people's heads staring

at the windows. The engines were throbbing through the deck like an electric saw grinding on a nail.

At first I thought the party chief decided it was either Bobby Joe or Skeeter and it was easier to hire a new shooter than a driller who had to keep a half-dozen other men who hated authority in line and make them like him for it at the same time.

But that evening, when I talked to Ray, the party chief, he cut right to it. So did I, just as soon as I found Bobby Joe up in his cabin, playing solitaire on his bunk, biting a white place on the corner of his lip.

"You sorry sonofabitch."

"I don't let a whole lot of people talk to me like that, W.J."

"He won't be able to work anywhere. That was a lousy thing to do, Bobby Joe."

"A man oughtn't have to work with a queer."

"You told Ray Skeeter came on to you?"

"How you know he didn't?"

" 'Cause I know you're a damn liar, Bobby Joe. I know you lied about Magpie cheating, too."

"You're in my light."

"Too bad. You're going to hear this," I said, and sat down on his bunk, right on top of his cards. His face twitched, like a rubber band snapping under the skin. Then I told him everything I knew about Skeeter, the coral rocks humming with the voices of Jap soldiers trapped down below, women with their babies dropping off the cliffs into the sea, all the guilt he was carrying around twelve years after we set fire to the air over their cities and had parades and got back down to making money.

"I ain't got nothing to say to you, W.J."

"I bet you ain't."

I was too hard on Bobby Joe, though. Two nights later he started acting weird, almost like Skeeter, paddling the pirogue out in the swamp, raking a pile of silt up on the paddle and staring at it, walking along the edge of a sandbar like he'd lost something while cicadas droned in the sky and the sun's last light looked like electric blood painted on the trees.

"The hurricane blew them sloughs slick as spit," I said to Bobby Joe.

"Where you figure Skeeter headed to?" he asked. He bit on his thumbnail and looked at it.

"Back to Wiggins, I expect."

"You think?"

"They'd know where he's at."

Bobby Joe drug up the next day, told Ray to mail his check general delivery, New Iberia, Louisiana. I never saw him or Skeeter again. But I sure heard about them; they must have been looking for each other all over the oil patch, one man trying to forgive the other so he could lay his own burden down.

Sometimes when it's hot and the barometer starts falling and the bottom of the sky turns green in the south, the way it does right before a storm, I start to think about Bobby Joe and Skeeter, or the girls in the hot-pillow joint who'd set up a drunk to get rolled, or the guys who didn't speak up when the party chief ran Skeeter off, and I commence to get a terrible headache, just like when you'd breathe that awful cloud of yellow smoke boiling off the water when we'd zap the juice into the hole and blow carp and catfish belly-up to the surface, never worrying about it or asking a question, like it was all a natural part of our old war with the earth and whatever was down there.

Texas City,

1947

Right after WW II everybody in southern Louisiana thought he was going to get rich in the oil business. My father convinced himself that all his marginal jobs in the oil fields would one day give him the capital to become an independent wildcatter, perhaps even a legendary figure like Houston's Glenn McCarthy, and he would successfully hammer together a drilling operation out of wooden towers and rusted junk, punch through the top of a geological dome, and blow salt water, sand, chains, pipe casing, and oil into the next parish.

So he worked on as a roughneck on drilling rigs and as

a jug-hustler with a seismograph outfit, then began contracting to build board roads in the marsh for the Texaco company. By mid-1946, he was actually leasing land in the Atchafalaya Basin and over in East Texas. But that was also the year that I developed rheumatic fever and he drove my mother off and brought Mattie home to live with us.

I remember the terrible fight they had the day she left. My mother had come home angry from her waitress job in a beer garden on that burning July afternoon, and without changing out of her pink dress with the white piping on the collar and pockets, she had begun butchering chickens on the stump in the backyard and shucking off their feathers in a big iron cauldron of scalding water. My father came home later than he should have, parked his pickup truck by the barn, and walked naked to the waist through the gate with his wadded-up shirt hanging out the back pocket of his Levi's. He was a dark Cajun, and his shoulders, chest, and back were streaked with black hair. He wore cowboy boots, a red sweat handkerchief tied around his neck, and a rakish straw hat that had an imitation snakeskin band around the crown.

Headless chickens were flopping all over the grass, and my mother's forearms were covered with wet chicken feathers. "I know you been with her. They were talking at the beer joint," she said, without looking up from where she sat with her knees apart on a wood chair in front of the steaming cauldron.

"I ain't been with nobody," he said, "except with them mosquitoes I been slapping out in that marsh."

"You said you'd leave her alone."

"You children go inside," my father said.

"That gonna make your conscience right 'cause you send them kids off, you? She gonna cut your throat one day. She been in the crazy house in Mandeville. You gonna see, Verise."

"I ain't seen her."

"You sonofabitch, I smell her on you," my mother said, and she swung a headless chicken by its feet and whipped a diagonal line of blood across my father's chest and Levi's.

"You ain't gonna act like that in front of my children, you," he said, and started toward her. Then he stopped. "Y'all get inside. You ain't got no business listening to this. This is between me and her."

My two older brothers, Weldon and Lyle, were used to our parents' quarrels, and they went inside sullenly and let the back screen slam behind them. But my little sister, Drew, whom my mother nicknamed "Little Britches," stood mute and fearful and alone under the pecan tree, her cat pressed flat against her chest.

"Come on, Drew. Come see inside. We're gonna play with the Monopoly game," I said, and tried to pull her by the arm. But her body was rigid, her bare feet immobile in the dust.

Then I saw my father's large, square hand go up in the air, saw it come down hard against the side of my mother's face, heard the sound of her weeping, as I tried to step into Drew's line of vision and hold her and her cat against my

body, hold the three of us tightly together outside the unrelieved sound of my mother's weeping.

Three hours later, her car went through the railing on
the bridge over the Atchafalaya River. I dreamed that night
that an enormous brown bubble rose from the submerged
wreck, and when it burst on the surface, her drowned breath
stuck against my face as wet and rank as gas released from a
grave.

≋

That fall I began to feel sick all the time, as though a gray
cloud of mosquitoes were feeding at my heart. During recess at school I didn't play with the other children and instead hung about on the edges of the dusty playground or,
when Brother Daniel wasn't looking, slipped around the
side of the old redbrick cathedral and sat by myself on a
stone bench in a bamboo-enclosed, oak-shaded garden
where a statue of Mary rested in a grotto and camellia
petals floated in a big goldfish pond. Sometimes Sister
Roberta was there saying her rosary.

She was built like a fire hydrant. Were it not for the ad-
ditional size that the swirl of her black habit and the wings
of her veil gave her, she would not have been much larger
than the students in her fifth-grade class. She didn't yell at
us or hit our knuckles with rulers like the other nuns did,
and in fact she always called us "little people" rather than
children. But sometimes her round face would flare with
anger below her white, starched wimple at issues which to

us, in our small parochial world, seemed of little impor-
tance. She told our class once that criminals and corrupt
local politicians were responsible for the slot and racehorse
machines that were in every drugstore, bar, and hotel lobby
in New Iberia, and another time she flung an apple core at
a carload of teenagers who were baiting the Negro janitor
out by the school incinerator.

She heard my feet on the dead oak leaves when I walked
through the opening in the bamboo into the garden. She was
seated on the stone bench, her back absolutely erect, the scarlet beads of her rosary stretched across the back of her pale
hand like drops of blood. She stopped her prayer and turned
her head toward me. Fine white hair grew on her upper lip.

"Do you feel sick again, Billy Bob?" she asked.

"Yes, Sister."

"Come here."

"What?"

"I said come here." Her hand reached out and held my
forehead. Then she wiped the moisture off her palm with
her fingers. "Have you been playing or running?"

"No, Sister."

"Has your father taken you to a doctor?"

I didn't answer.

"Look at me and answer my question," she said.

"He don't—he doesn't have money right now. He says
it's because I had the flu. He boiled some honey and onions
for me to eat. It made me feel better. It's true, Sister."

"I need to talk to your father."

She saw me swallow.

"Would he mind my calling him?" she asked.

"He's not home now. He works all the time."

"Will he be home tonight?"

"I'm not sure."

"Who takes care of you at night when he's not home?"

"A lady, a friend of his."

"I see. Come back to the classroom with me. It's too windy out here for you," she said.

"Sister, you don't need to call, do you? I feel okay now. My father's got a lot on his mind now. He works real hard."

"What's wrong in your house, Billy Bob?"

"Nothing. I promise, Sister." I tried to smile. I could taste bile in my throat.

"Don't lie."

"I'm not. I promise I'm not."

"Yes, I can see that clearly. Come with me."

The rest of the recess period she and I sharpened crayons in the empty room with tiny pencil sharpeners, stringing long curlicues of colored wax into the wastebasket. She was as silent and as seemingly self-absorbed as a statue. Just before the bell rang she walked down to the convent and came back with a tube of toothpaste.

"Your breath is bad. Go down to the lavatory and wash your mouth out with this," she said.

≋

Mattie wore shorts and sleeveless blouses with sweat rings under the arms, and in the daytime she always seemed to have curlers in her hair. When she walked from room to room she carried an ashtray with her into which she constantly flicked her lipstick-stained Chesterfields. She had a hard, muscular body, and she didn't close the bathroom door all the way when she bathed, and once I saw her kneeling in the tub, scrubbing her big shoulders and chest with a large, flat brush. The area above her head was crisscrossed with improvised clotheslines from which dripped her wet underthings. Her eyes fastened on mine; I thought she was about to reprimand me for staring at her, but instead her hard-boned, shiny face continued to look back at me with a vacuous indifference that made me feel obscene.

If my father was out of town on a Friday or Saturday night, she fixed our supper (sometimes meat on Friday, the fear in our eyes not worthy of her recognition), put on her blue suit, and sat by herself in the living room, listening to the Grand Ole Opry or the Louisiana Hayride, while she drank apricot brandy from a coffee cup. She always dropped cigarette ashes on her suit and had to spot-clean the cloth with dry cleaning fluid before she drove off for the evening in her old Ford coupe. I don't know where she went on those Friday or Saturday nights, but a boy down the road told me that Mattie used to work in Broussard's Bar on Railroad Avenue, an infamous area in New Iberia where the women sat on the galleries of the cribs, dipping their beer out of buckets and yelling at the railroad and oil-field workers in the street.

Then one morning when my father was in Morgan City, a man in a new silver Chevrolet sedan came out to see her. It was hot, and he parked his car partly on our grass to keep it in the shade. He wore sideburns, striped brown zoot slacks, two-tone shoes, suspenders, a pink shirt without a coat, and a fedora that shadowed his narrow face. While he talked to her, he put one shoe on the car bumper and wiped the dust off it with a rag. Then their voices grew louder and he said, "You like the life. Admit it, you. He ain't given you no wedding ring, has he? You don't buy the cow, no, when you can milk through the fence."

"I am currently involved with a gentleman. I do not know what you are talking about. I am not interested in anything you are talking about," she said.

He threw the rag back inside the car and opened the car door. "It's always trick, trade, or travel, darlin'," he said. "Same rules here as down on Railroad. He done made you a nigger woman for them children, Mattie."

"Are you calling me a nigra?" she said quietly.

"No, I'm calling you crazy, just like everybody say you are. No, I take that back, me. I ain't calling you nothing. I ain't got to, 'cause you gonna be back. You in the life, Mattie. You be phoning me to come out here, bring you to the crib, rub your back, put some of that warm stuff in your arm again. Ain't nobody else do that for you, huh?"

When she came back into the house, she made us take all the dishes out of the cabinets, even though they were clean, and wash them over again.

It was the following Friday that Sister Roberta called. Mattie was already dressed to go out. She didn't bother to turn down the radio when she answered the phone, and in order to compete with Red Foley's voice, she had to almost shout into the receiver.

"Mr. Sonnier is not here," she said. "Mr. Sonnier is away on business in Texas City . . . No, ma'am, I'm not the housekeeper. I'm a friend of the family who is caring for these children . . . There's nothing wrong with that boy that I can see . . . Are you calling to tell me that there's something wrong, that I'm doing something wrong? What is it that I'm doing wrong? I would like to know that. What is your name?"

I stood transfixed with terror in the hall as she bent angrily into the mouthpiece and her knuckles ridged on the receiver. A storm was blowing in from the Gulf, the air smelled of ozone, and the southern horizon was black with thunderclouds that pulsated with white veins of lightning. I heard the wind ripping through the trees in the yard and pecans rattling down on the gallery roof like grapeshot.

When Mattie hung up the phone, the skin of her face was stretched as tight as a lamp shade and one liquid eye was narrowed at me like someone aiming down a rifle barrel.

〰〰

The next week, when I was cutting through the neighbor's sugarcane field on the way home from school, my heart started to race for no reason, my spit tasted like pecans, and my face filmed with perspiration even though the wind was cool through the stalks of cane; then I saw the oaks and cypress trees along Bayou Teche tilt at an angle, and I dropped my books and fell forward in the dirt as though someone had wrapped a chain around my chest and snapped my breastbone.

I lay with the side of my face pressed against the dirt, my mouth gasping like a fish's, until Weldon found me and went crashing through the cane for help. A doctor came out to the house that night, examined me and gave me a shot, then talked with my father out in the hall. My father didn't understand the doctor's vocabulary, and he said, "What kind of fever that is?"

"Rheumatic, Mr. Sonnier. It attacks the heart. I could be wrong, but I think that's what your boy's got. I'll be back tomorrow."

"How much this gonna cost?"

"It's three dollars for the visit, but you can pay me when you're able."

"We never had nothing like this in our family. You sure about this?"

"No, I'm not. That's why I'll be back. Good night to you, sir."

I knew he didn't like my father, but he came to see me one afternoon a week for a month, brought me bottles of medicine, and always looked into my face with genuine concern after he listened to my heart. Then one night he and my father argued and he didn't come back.

"What good he do, huh?" my father said. "You still

sick, ain't you? A doctor don't make money off well people. I think maybe you got malaria, son. There ain't nothing for that, either. It just goes away. You gonna see, you.
You stay in bed, you eat cush-cush Mattie and me make for
you, you drink that Hadacol vitamin tonic, you wear this
dime I'm tying on you, you gonna get well and go back to
school."

He hung a perforated dime on a piece of red twine
around my neck. His face was lean and unshaved, his eyes
as intense as a butane flame when he looked into mine.
"You blame me for your mama?" he asked.

"No, sir," I lied.

"I didn't mean to hit her. But she made me look bad in
front of y'all. A woman can't be doing that to a man in
front of his kids."

"Make Mattie go away, Daddy."

"Don't be saying that."

"She hit Weldon with the belt. She made Drew kneel in
the bathroom corner because she didn't flush the toilet."

"She's just trying to be a mother, that's all. Don't talk no
more. Go to sleep. I got to drive back to Texas City tonight.
You gonna be all right."

He closed my door and the inside of my room was absolutely black. Through the wall I heard him and Mattie
talking, then the weight of their bodies creaking rhythmi-
cally on the bedsprings.

When Sister Roberta knew that I would not be back to school that semester, she began bringing my lessons to the house. She came three afternoons a week and had to walk two miles each way between the convent and our house. Each time I successfully completed a lesson she rewarded me with a holy card. Each holy card had a prayer on one side and a beautiful picture on the other, usually of angels and saints glowing with light or ethereal paintings of Mary with the Infant Jesus. On the day after my father had tied the dime around my neck, Sister Roberta had to walk past our neighbor's field right after he had cut his cane and burned off the stubble, and a wet wind had streaked her black habit with ashes. As soon as she came through my bedroom door her face tightened inside her wimple, and her brown eyes, which had flecks of red in them, grew round and hot. She dropped her book bag on the foot of my bed and leaned within six inches of my face as though she were looking down at a horrid presence in the bottom of a well. The hair on her upper lip looked like pieces of silver thread.

"Who put that around your neck?" she asked.

"My father says it keeps the gris-gris away."

"My suffering God," she said, and went back out the door in a swirl of cloth. Then I heard her speak to Mattie: "That's right, madam. Scissors. So I can remove that cord from his neck before he strangles to death in his sleep. Thank you kindly."

She came back into my bedroom, pulled the twine out from my throat with one finger, and snipped it in two. "Do you believe in this nonsense, Billy Bob?" she said.

"No, Sister."

"That's good. You're a good Catholic boy, and you mustn't believe in superstition. Do you love the church?"

"I think so."

"Hmmmm. That doesn't sound entirely convincing. Do you love your father?"

"I don't know."

"I see. Do you love your sister and your brothers?"

"Yes. Most of the time I do."

"That's good. Because if you love somebody, or if you love the church, like I do, then you don't ever have to be afraid. People are only superstitious when they're afraid. That's an important lesson for little people to learn. Now, let's take a look at our math test for this week."

Over her shoulder I saw Mattie looking at us from the living room, her hair in foam rubber curlers, her face contorted as though a piece of barbed wire were twisting behind her eyes.

≈≈≈

That winter my father started working regular hours, what he called "an indoor job," at the Monsanto Chemical Company in Texas City, and we saw him only on weekends. Mattie cooked only the evening meal and made us responsible for the care of the house and the other two meals. Weldon started to get into trouble at school. His eighth-grade teacher, a laywoman, called and said he had thumb-tacked a girl's dress to the desk during class, causing her to almost tear it off her body when the bell rang, and he would either pay for the dress or be suspended. Mattie hung up the phone on her, and two days later the girl's father, a sheriff's deputy, came out to the house and made Mattie give him four dollars on the gallery.

She came back inside, slamming the door, her face burning, grabbed Weldon by the collar of his T-shirt, and walked him into the backyard, where she made him stand for two hours on an upended apple crate until he wet his pants.

Later, after she had let him come back inside and he had changed his underwear and blue jeans, he went outside into the dark by himself, without eating supper, and sat on the butcher stump, striking kitchen matches on the side of the box and throwing them at the chickens. Before we went to sleep he sat for a long time on the side of his bed, next to mine, in a square of moonlight with his hands balled into fists on his thighs. There were knots of muscle in the backs of his arms and behind his ears. Mattie had given him a burr haircut, and his head looked as hard and scalped as a baseball.

"Tomorrow's Saturday. We're going to listen to the LSU-Rice game," I said.

"Some colored kids saw me from the road and laughed."

"I don't care what they did. You're brave, Weldon. You're braver than any of us."

"I'm gonna fix her."

His voice made me afraid. The branches of the pecan trees were skeletal, like gnarled fingers against the moon.

"Don't be thinking like that," I said. "It'll just make her do worse things. She takes it out on Drew when you and Lyle aren't here."

"Go to sleep, Billy Bob," he said. His eyes were wet. "She hurts us because we let her. We ax for it. You get hurt when you don't stand up. Just like Momma did."

I heard him snuffling in the dark. Then he lay down with his face turned toward the opposite wall. His head looked carved out of gray wood in the moonlight.

≈≈≈

I went back to school for the spring semester. Maybe because of the balmy winds off the Gulf and the heavy, fecund smell of magnolia and wisteria on the night air, I wanted to believe that a new season was beginning in my heart as well. I couldn't control what happened at home, but the school was a safe place, one where Sister Roberta ruled her little fifth-grade world like an affectionate despot.

I was always fascinated by her hands. They were like toy hands, small as a child's, as pink as an early rose, the nails not much bigger than pearls. She was wonderful at sketching and drawing with crayons and colored chalk. In minutes she could create a beautiful religious scene on the blackboard to fit the church's season, but she also drew pictures for us of Easter rabbits and talking Easter eggs. Sometimes she would draw only the outline of a figure—an archangel with enormous wings, a Roman soldier about to be dazzled by a blinding light—and she would let us take turns coloring in the solid areas. She told us the secret to great classroom art was to always keep your chalk and crayons pointy.

Then we began to hear rumors about Sister Roberta, of a kind that we had never heard about any of the nuns, who all seemed to have no lives other than the ones that were immediately visible to us. She had been heard weeping in the confessional, she had left the convent for three days without permission, two detectives from Baton Rouge had questioned her in the Mother Superior's office.

She missed a week of school and a lay teacher took her place. She returned for two weeks, then was gone again. When she came back the second time she was soft-spoken and removed, and sometimes she didn't even bother to answer simple questions that we asked her. She would gaze out the window for long periods, as though her attention were fixed on a distant object, then a noise—a creaking desk, an eraser flung from the cloakroom—would disturb her, and her eyes would return to the room, absolutely empty of thought or meaning.

I stayed after school on a Friday to help her wash the blackboards and pound erasers.

"You don't need to, Billy Bob. The janitor will take care of it," she said, staring idly out the window.

"All the kids like you, Sister," I said.

"What?" she said.

"You're the only one who plays with us at recess. You don't ever get mad at us, either. Not for real, anyway."

"It's nice of you to say that, but the other sisters are good to you, too."

"Not like you are."

"You shouldn't talk to me like that, Billy Bob." She had lost weight, and there was a solitary crease, like a line drawn by a thumbnail, in each of her cheeks.

"It's wrong for you to be sad," I said.

"You must run along home now. Don't say anything more."

I wish you were my mother, I thought I heard myself say inside my head.

"What did you say?" she asked.

"Nothing."

"Tell me what you said."

"I don't think I said anything. I really don't think I did."

My heart was beating against my rib cage, the same way it had the day I fell unconscious in the sugarcane field.

"Billy Bob, don't try to understand the world. It's not ours to understand," she said. "You must give up the things you can't change. You mustn't talk to me like this anymore. You—"

But I was already racing from the room, my soul painted with an unrelieved shame that knew no words.

≈≈≈

The next week I found out the source of Sister Roberta's grief. A strange and seedy man by the name of Mr. Trajan, who always had an American flag pin on his lapel when you saw him inside the wire cage of the grocery and package store he operated by the Negro district, had cut an article from copies of the Baton Rouge *Morning Advocate* and the Lafayette *Daily Advertiser* and mailed it to other Catholic businessmen in town. An eighth-grader who had been held back twice, once by Sister Roberta, brought it to school one day, and after the three o'clock bell Lyle, Weldon, and I heard him reading it to a group of dumbfounded boys on the playground. The words hung in the air like our first exposure to God's name being deliberately used in vain.

Her brother had killed a child, and Sister Roberta had helped him hide in a fishing camp in West Baton Rouge Parish.

"Give me that," Weldon said, and tore the news article out of the boy's hand. He stared hard at it, then wadded it up and threw it on the ground. "Get the fuck out of here. You go around talking about this again and I'll kick your ass."

"That's right, you dumb fuck," Lyle said, putting his new baseball cap in his back pocket and setting his book satchel down by his foot.

"That's right, butt face," I added, incredulous at the boldness of my own words.

"Yeah?" the boy said, but the resolve in his voice was already breaking.

"Yeah!" Weldon said, and shoved him off balance. Then he picked up a rock and chased the boy and three of his friends toward the street. Lyle and I followed, picking up

dirt clods in our hands. When the boy was almost to his father's waiting pickup truck, he turned and shot us the finger. Weldon nailed him right above the eye with the rock.

One of the brothers marched us down to Father Higgins's office and left us there to wait for Father Higgins,
whose razor strop and black-Irish, crimson-faced tirades
were legendary in the school. The office smelled of the
cigar butts in the wastebasket and the cracked leather in the
chairs. A walnut pendulum clock ticked loudly on the wall.
It was overcast outside, and we sat in the gloom and silence
until four o'clock.

"I ain't waiting anymore. Y'all coming?" Weldon said,
and put one leg out the open window.

"You'll get expelled," I said.

"Too bad. I ain't going to wait around just to have
somebody whip me," he said, and dropped out the window.

Five minutes later, Lyle followed him.

The sound of the clock was like a spoon knocking on a
hollow wood box. When Father Higgins finally entered the
room, he was wearing his horn-rimmed glasses and thumb-
ing through a sheaf of papers attached to a clipboard. The
hairline on the back of his neck was shaved neatly with a
razor. At first he seemed distracted by my presence, then he
flipped the sheets of paper to a particular page, almost as an
afterthought, and studied it. He put an unlit cigar stub in his
mouth, looked at me, then back at the page.

"You threw a rock at somebody?" he said.

"No, Father."

"Somebody threw a rock at you?"

"I wouldn't say that."

"Then what are you doing here?"

"I don't know," I replied.

"That's interesting. All right, since you don't know why you're here, how about going somewhere else?"

"I'll take him, Father," I heard Sister Roberta say in the doorway. She put her hand on my arm, walked me down the darkly polished corridor to the breezeway outside, then sat me down on the stone bench inside the bamboo-enclosed garden where she often said her rosary.

She sat next to me, her small white hands curved on the edges of the bench, and looked down at the goldfish pond while she talked. A crushed paper cup floated among the hyacinth leaves. "You meant well, Billy Bob, but I don't want you to defend me anymore. It's not the job of little people to defend adults."

"Sister, the newspaper said–"

"It said what?"

"You were in trouble with the police. Can they put you in jail?"

She put her hand on top of mine. Her fingernails looked like tiny pink seashells. "They're not really interested in me, Billy Bob. My brother is an alcoholic, and he killed a little boy with his car, then he ran away. But they probably won't send my brother to prison because the child was a Negro." Her hand was hot and damp on top of mine. Her voice clicked wetly in her throat. "He'll be spared, not because he's a sick man, but because it was a colored child he killed."

When I looked at her again, her long eyelashes were bright with tears. She stood up with her face turned away from me. The sun had broken through the gray seal of clouds, and the live oak tree overhead was filled with the clattering of mockingbirds and blue jays. I felt her tiny fingernails rake gently through my hair, as though she were combing a cat.

"Oh, you poor child, you have lice eggs in your hair," she said. Then she pressed my head against her breast, and I felt her tears strike hotly on the back of my neck.

≈≈≈

Three days later, Sister saw the cigarette burn on Drew's leg in the lunchroom and reported it to the social welfare agency in town. A consumptive rail of a man in a dandruff-flecked blue suit drove out to the house and questioned Mattie on the gallery, then questioned us in front of her. Drew told him she had been burned by an ember that had popped out of a trash fire in the backyard.

He raised her chin with his knuckle. His black hair was stiff with grease. "Is that what happened?" he asked.

"Yes, sir." Drew's face was dull, her mouth downturned at the corners. The burn was scabbed now and looked like a tightly coiled gray worm on her skin.

He smiled and took his knuckle away from her chin. "Then you shouldn't play next to the fire," he said.

"I would like to know who sent you out here," Mattie said.

"That's confidential." He coughed on the back of his hand. His shirt cuff was frayed and for some reason looked particularly pretentious and sad on his thin wrist. "And to tell you the truth, I don't really know. My supervisor didn't tell me. I guess that's how the chain of command works." He coughed again, this time loud and hard, and I could smell the nicotine that was buried in his lungs. "But everything here looks all right. Perhaps this is much ado about nothing. Not a bad day for a drive, though."

Weldon's eyes were as hard as marbles, but he didn't speak.

The man walked with Mattie to his car, and I felt like doors were slamming all around us. She put her foot on his running board and propped one arm on his car roof while she talked, so that her breasts were uplifted against her blouse and her dress made a loop between her legs.

"Let's tell him," Lyle said.

"Are you kidding? Look at him. He'd eat her shit with a spoon," Weldon said.

〰〰〰

It was right after first period the next morning that we heard about the disaster at Texas City. Somebody shouted something about it on the playground, then suddenly the whole school was abuzz with rumors. Cars on the street pulled to the curb with their radios tuned to news stations, and we could even hear the principal's old boxwood radio blaring through the open window upstairs. A ship loaded with fertilizer had been burning in the harbor, and while people on the docks had watched firefighting boats pumping geysers of water onto the ship's decks, the fire had dripped into the hold. The explosion filled the sky with rockets of smoke and rained an umbrella of flame down on the Monsanto chemical plant. The force of the secondary explosion was so great that it blew out windows in Houston, fifty miles away. But it wasn't over yet. The fireball mushroomed laterally out into an adjacent oil field, and rows of storage tanks and wellheads went like strings of Chinese firecrackers. People said the water in the harbor boiled from the heat, the spars on steel derricks melting like licorice.

We heard nothing about the fate of my father either that afternoon or evening. Mattie got drunk that night and fell asleep in the living-room chair by the radio. I felt nothing about my father's possible death, and I wondered at my own callousness. We went to school the next morning, and when we returned home in the afternoon Mattie was waiting on the gallery to tell us that a man from the Monsanto Company had telephoned and said that my father was listed as missing. Her eyes were pink with either hangover or crying, and her face was puffy and round, like a white balloon.

When we didn't respond, she said, "Your father may be dead. Do you understand what I'm saying? That was an important man from his company who called. He would not call unless he was gravely concerned. Do you children understand what is being said to you?"

Weldon brushed at the dirt with his tennis shoe, and
Lyle looked into a place about six inches in front of his
eyes. Drew's face was frightened, not because of the news
about our father, but instead because of the strange
whirring of wheels that we could almost hear from inside
Mattie's head. I put my arm over her shoulders and felt her
skin jump.

"He's worked like a nigra for you, maybe lost his life for
you, and you have nothing to say?" Mattie asked.

"Maybe we ought to start cleaning up our rooms. You
wanted us to clean up our rooms, Mattie," I said.

But it was a poor attempt to placate her.

"You stay outside. Don't even come in this house," she
said.

"I have to go to the bathroom," Lyle said.

"Then you can just do it in the dirt like a darky," she
said, and went inside the house and latched the screen behind her.

≈≈≈

By the next afternoon, my father was still unaccounted for.
Mattie had an argument on the phone with somebody, I
think the man in zoot pants and two-tone shoes who had
probably been her pimp at one time, because she told him
he owed her money and she wouldn't come back and work
at Broussard's Bar again until he paid her. After she hung
up she breathed hard at the kitchen sink, smoking her cigarette and staring out into the yard. She snapped the cap off

a bottle of Jax and drank it half empty, her throat working in one long, wet swallow, one eye cocked at me.

"Come here," she said.

"What?"

"You tracked up the kitchen. You didn't flush the toilet after you used it, either."

"I did."

"You did what?"

"I flushed the toilet."

"Then one of the others didn't flush it. Every one of you come out here. Now!"

"What is it, Mattie? We didn't do anything," I said.

"I changed my mind. Every one of you outside. All of you outside. Weldon and Lyle, you get out there right now. Where's Drew?"

"She's playing in the yard. What's wrong, Mattie?" I made no attempt to hide the fear in my voice. I could see the web of blue veins in the top of her muscular chest.

Outside, the wind was blowing through the trees in the yard, flattening the purple clumps of wisteria that grew against the barn wall.

"Each of you go to the hedge and cut the switch you want me to use on you," she said.

It was her favorite form of punishment for us. If we broke off a large switch, she hit us fewer times with it. If we came back with a thin or small switch, we would get whipped until she felt she had struck some kind of balance between size and number.

We remained motionless. Drew had been playing with

her cat. She had tied a piece of twine around the cat's neck, and she held the twine in her hand like a leash. Her knees and white socks were dusty from play.

"I told you not to tie that around the kitten's neck again," Mattie said.

"It doesn't hurt anything. It's not your cat, anyway," Weldon said.

"Don't sass me," she said. "You will not sass me. None of you will sass me."

"I ain't cutting no switch," Weldon said. "You're crazy. My mama said so. You ought to be in the crazy house."

She looked hard into Weldon's eyes, then there was a moment of recognition in her colorless face, a flicker of fear, as though she had seen a growing meanness of spirit in Weldon that would soon become a challenge to her own. She wet her lips.

"We shall see who does what around here," she said. She broke off a big switch from the myrtle hedge and raked it free of flowers and leaves, except for one green sprig on the tip.

I saw the look in Drew's face, saw her drop the piece of twine from her palm as she stared up into Mattie's shadow.

Mattie jerked her by the wrist and whipped her a half-dozen times across her bare legs. Drew twisted impotently in Mattie's balled hand, her feet dancing with each blow. The switch raised welts on her skin as thick and red as centipedes.

Then suddenly Weldon ran with all his weight into Mattie's back, stiff-arming her between the shoulder blades, and sent her tripping sideways over a bucket of chicken slops. She righted herself and stared at him openmouthed, the switch limp in her hand. Then her eyes grew hot and bright, and I could see the bone flex along her jaws.

Weldon burst out the back gate and ran down the dirt road between the sugarcane fields, the soles of his dirty tennis shoes powdering dust in the air.

She waited for him a long time, watching through the screen as the mauve-colored dusk gathered in the trees and the sun's afterglow lit the clouds on the western horizon. Then she took a bottle of apricot brandy into the bathroom and sat in the tub for almost an hour, turning the hot water tap on and off until the tank was empty. When we needed to go to the bathroom, she told us to take our problem outside. Finally she emerged in the hall, wearing only her panties and bra, her hair wrapped in a towel, the dark outline of her sex plainly visible to us.

"I'm going to dress now and go into town with a gentleman friend," she said. "Tomorrow we're going to start a new regime around here. Believe me, there will never be a reoccurrence of what happened here today. You can pass that on to young Mr. Weldon for me."

But she didn't go into town. Instead, she put on her blue suit, a flower-print blouse, her nylon stockings, and walked up and down on the gallery, her cigarette poised in the air like a movie actress.

"Why not just drive your car, Mattie?" I said quietly through the screen.

"It has no gas. Besides, a gentleman caller will be passing for me anytime now," she answered.

"Oh."

She blew smoke at an upward angle, her face aloof and flat-sided in the shadows.

"Mattie?"

"Yes?"

"Weldon's out back. Can he come in the house?"

"Little mice always return where the cheese is," she said.

I hated her. I wanted something terrible to happen to her. I could feel my fingernails knifing into my palms.

She turned around, her palm supporting one elbow, her cigarette an inch from her mouth, her hair wreathed in smoke. "Do you have a reason for staring through the screen at me?" she asked.

"No," I said.

"When you're bigger, you'll get to do what's on your mind. In the meantime, don't let your thoughts show on your face. You're a lewd little boy."

Her suggestion repelled me and made water well up in my eyes. I backed away from the screen, then turned and ran through the rear of the house and out into the backyard where Weldon, Lyle, and Drew sat against the barn wall, fireflies lighting in the wisteria over their heads.

No one came for Mattie that evening. She sat in the stuffed chair in her room, putting on layers of lipstick until her mouth had the crooked, bright red shape of a clown's. She smoked a whole package of Chesterfields, constantly wiping the ashes off her dark blue skirt with a hand towel soaked in dry cleaning fluid; then she drank herself unconscious.

It was hot that night, and dry lightning leaped from the horizon to the top of the blue-black vault of sky over the Gulf. Weldon sat on the side of his bed in the dark, his shoulders hunched, his fists between his white thighs. His burr haircut looked like duck down on his head in the flicker of lightning through the window. When I was almost asleep he shook both me and Lyle awake and said, "We got to get rid of her. You know we got to do it."

I put my pillow over my head and rolled away from him, as though I could drop away into sleep and rise in the morning into a sun-spangled and different world.

But in the false dawn I woke to both Lyle's and Weldon's faces close to mine. Weldon's eyes were hollow, his breath rank with funk. The mist was heavy and wet in the pecan trees outside the window.

"She's not gonna hurt Drew again. Are you gonna help or not?" Weldon said.

I followed them into the hallway, my heart sinking at the realization of what I was willing to participate in, my body as numb as if I had been stunned with novocaine. Mattie was sleeping in the stuffed chair, her hose rolled down over her knees, an overturned jelly glass on the rug next to the can of spot cleaner.

Weldon walked quietly across the rug, unscrewed the cap on the can, laid the can on its side in front of Mattie's feet, then backed away from her. The cleaning fluid spread in a dark circle around her chair, the odor as bright and sharp as a slap across the face.

Weldon slid open a box of kitchen matches and we each took one, raked it across the striker, and, with the sense that our lives at that moment had changed forever, threw them at Mattie's feet. But the burning matches fell outside the wet area. The blood veins in my head dilated with fear, my ears hummed with a sound like the roar of the ocean in a seashell, and I jerked the box from Weldon's hand, clutched a half-dozen matches in my fist, dragged them across the striker, and flung them right on Mattie's feet.

The chair was enveloped in a cone of flame, and she burst out of it with her arms extended, as though she were pushing blindly through a curtain, her mouth and eyes wide with terror. We could smell her hair burning as she raced past us and crashed through the screen door out onto the gallery and into the yard. She beat at her flaming clothes and raked at her hair as though it were swarming with yellow jackets.

I stood transfixed in mortal dread at what I had done.

A Negro man walking to work came out of the mist on the road and knocked her to the ground, slapping the fire out of her dress, pinning her under his spread knees as though he were assaulting her. Smoke rose from her scorched clothes and hair as in a depiction of a damned figure on one of my holy cards.

The Negro rose to his feet and walked toward the gallery, a solitary line of blood running down his cheek where Mattie had scratched him.

"Yo' mama ain't hurt bad. Get some butter or some bacon grease. She gonna be all right, you gonna see. You children don't be worried, no," he said. His gums were purple with snuff when he smiled.

The volunteer firemen bounced across the cattle guard in an old fire truck whose obsolete hand-crank starter still dangled from under the radiator. They coated Mattie's room with foam from a fire extinguisher and packed Mattie off in an ambulance to the charity hospital in Lafayette. Two sheriff's deputies arrived, and before he left, one of the volunteers took them aside in the yard and talked with them, looking over his shoulder at us children, then walked over to us and said, "The fire chief gonna come out here and check it out. Y'all stay out of that bedroom."

His face was narrow and dark with shadow under the brim of his big rubber fireman's hat. I felt a fist squeeze my heart.

But suddenly Sister Roberta was in the midst of everything. Someone had carried word to the school about the fire, and she'd had one of the brothers drive her out to the house. She talked with the deputies, helped us fix cereal at the kitchen table, and made telephone calls to find a place for us to stay besides the welfare shelter. Then she looked in Mattie's bedroom door and studied the interior for what seemed a long time. When she came back in the kitchen, her eyes peeled the skin off our faces. I looked straight down into my cereal bowl.

She placed her small hand on my shoulder. I could feel

her fingers tapping on the bone, as though she were processing her own thoughts. Then she said, "Well, what should we do here today? I think we should clean up first. Where's the broom?"

Without waiting for an answer she pulled the broom out of the closet and went to work in Mattie's room, sweeping the spilled and unstruck matches as well as the burned ones in a pile by a side door that gave onto the yard. The soot and blackened threads from the rug swirled up in a cloud around her veils and wings and smudged her starched wimple.

One of the deputies put his hand on the broomstick. "There ain't been an investigation yet. You can't do that till the fire chief come out and see, Sister," he said.

"You always talked like a fool, Gaspard," she said. "Now that you have a uniform, you talk like a bigger one. This house smells like an incinerator. Now get out of the way." With one sweep of the broom she raked all the matches out into the yard.

≋

We were placed in foster homes, and over the years I lost contact with Sister Roberta. But later I went to work in the oil fields, and I think perhaps I talked with my father in a nightclub outside of Morgan City. An enormous live oak tree grew through the floor and roof, and he was leaning against the bar that had been built in a circle around the tree. His face was puckered with white scar tissue, his ears burnt into stubs, his right hand atrophied and frozen against his chest like a broken bird's foot. But beyond the layers of mutilated skin I could see my father's face, like the image in a photographic negative held up against a light.

"Is your name Sonnier?" I asked.

He looked at me curiously.

"Maybe. You want to buy me a drink?" he said.

"Yeah, I can do that," I said.

He ordered a shot of Beam with a frosted schooner of Jax on the side.

"Are you Verise Sonnier from New Iberia?" I asked.

He grinned stiffly when he took the schooner of beer away from his mouth. "Why you want to know?" he said.

"I think I'm your son. I'm Billy Bob."

His turquoise eyes wandered over my face, then they lost interest.

"I had a son. But you ain't him. Buy me another shot?" he said.

"Why not?" I replied.

Sometimes he comes to me in my dreams, and I wonder if ironically all our stories were written on his skin back there in Texas City in 1947. Or maybe that's just a poetic illusion purchased by time. But even in the middle of an Indian summer's day, when the sugarcane is beaten with purple and gold light in the fields and the sun is both warm and cool on your skin at the same time, when I know that the earth is a fine place after all, I have to mourn just a moment for those people of years ago who lived lives they did not choose, who carried burdens that were not their own, whose invisible scars were as private as the scarlet beads of Sister Roberta's rosary wrapped across the back of her small hand, as bright as drops of blood ringed round the souls of little people.

Mist

≈≈≈≈≈≈≈≈≈≈≈≈≈≈≈≈≈≈≈≈≈≈≈≈≈≈≈≈≈≈≈

≈≈≈≈≈≈≈≈≈ **L**isa Guillory's dreams are indistinct and do
≈≈≈≈≈≈≈≈≈ not contain the images normally associated
with nightmares. Nor do dawn and the early-morning mist
in the trees come to her in either the form of release or ex-
pectation. Instead, her dreams seem to be without sharp
edges, like the dull pain of an impacted tooth that takes up
nightly residence in her sleep and denies her rest but does
not terrify or cause her to wake with night sweats, as is the
case with many people at the meetings she has started at-
tending.

The meetings are held in a wood-frame Pentecostal

church that is set back in a sugarcane field lined with long rows of cane stubble the farmers burn off at night. In the morning, as she drives to the meeting from the shotgun cabin in what is called the Loreauville "quarters," where she now lives, the two-lane is thick with smoke from the stubble fires and the fog rolling off Bayou Teche. She can smell the ash and the burned soil and the heavy, fecund odor of the bayou inside the fog, but it is the fog itself that bothers her, not the odor, because in truth she does not want to leave it and the comfort it seems to provide her.

She pulls to the shoulder of the road and lights a cigarette, inhaling it deeply into her lungs, as though a cigarette can keep at bay the desires, no, the cravings, that build inside her throughout the day, until she imagines that a loop of piano wire has been fitted around her head and is being twisted into her scalp.

Lisa's sponsor is Tookie Goula. She is waiting for Lisa like a gargoyle by the entrance to the clapboard church. Tookie takes one look at Lisa's face and tells her she has to come clean in front of the group, that the time of silent participation has passed, that she has a serious illness and she has to get rid of shame and guilt and admit she is setting herself up for a relapse.

Lisa feigns indifference and boredom. She has heard it all before. "Talking at the meeting gonna get that knocking sound out of my head?"

"What's the knocking sound mean, Lisa?"

"It means he was rocking around inside the coffin when

they carried him to the graveyard. I heard it. Like rocks rolling 'round inside a barrel."

Tookie is a thick-bodied Cajun woman with jailhouse tats and a stare like a slap. She is not only inured to financial hardship and worthless men but she did a stint as a prostitute in a chain of truck stops across the upper South. She wears no makeup, bites her nails when she is angry, and doesn't hide the fact she probably likes women more than men. She is chewing on a nail now, her eyes hot as BBs. "Quit lying," she says.

Lisa can feel the heat bloom in her chest. She tries to slip into the role of victim. "Why you want to hurt me like that?"

" 'Cause you ain't honest. 'Cause you ain't gonna get well till you stop jerking yourself around," Tookie replies.

"The army didn't want me to see what he looked like. All of him wasn't in the coffin. Maybe it wasn't even him," Lisa says.

"You like making yourself suffer?"

Lisa thinks she is going to break down. She wants to break her fists on Tookie's face.

"You're setting yourself up to use, girl," Tookie says. "You're gonna see Herman Stanga. I know your t'oughts before you have them."

"Least I ain't got to wear tattoos to hide the needle scars on my arms," Lisa says. "Least I don't wake up in the morning wondering what gender I am."

During the meeting Tookie keeps raising her dark eyes to Lisa's, biting on her nails, rubbing the powerful muscles in her forearms, breathing with a sound like sand sliding down a drainpipe. Lisa can't take it anymore. "My husband got killed nort' of Baghdad. I know I'm suppose to work on acceptance, but it's hard," she blurts out, without introducing herself by name or identifying herself as an alcoholic or an addict. "I got twenty-seven days now. But I start t'inking of Gerald and how he died and what he must have looked like before they shipped him home, and I start having real bad t'oughts. 'Bout scoring a li'l bit of rock, maybe, not much, just a taste. Like maybe I can still handle it. I'm saying these t'ings 'cause my sponsor says I got to get honest."

She had believed her statement about her loss would suck the air out of the room and fill her listeners with shock and sympathy and in the ensuing silence make Tookie regret her callousness. But the local National Guard unit lost five members in Iraq in one day alone and no one has a patent now on stories of wounded and maimed and dead GIs from South Louisiana. In fact, if anything, Lisa's admission seems either to antagonize or bore those who are not staring out the window, trapped inside their own desperation and ennui. She realizes that in her self-absorption she has interrupted a woman who has recently been gang-raped in a crack house. Her cheeks burn with embarrassment.

"I'm sorry," she says. "My name is Lisa. I'm an alcoholic and a drug addict."

"Keep coming back, Lisa. Those first ninety days are a rough gig. Sometimes you got to fake it till you make it," the chair of the meeting, a white man, says. Then he calls on someone else as though flipping a page in a book.

Fake it till you make it? Fake what? Being sick all the time?

After the meeting she heads straight for her car, looking neither to the right nor to the left, but Tookie inserts herself like an attack dog in her path. "What was that pity-pot stuff about?"

"I made a fool of myself. You ain't got to tell me," Lisa replies.

Tookie's eyes try to peel the skin off Lisa's face. "There's something you ain't owned up to," she says.

"My husband got blown apart. What else I got to tell you?"

"That was eight months ago. What you hiding, you? What happened in New Orleans?"

The sunshine is cold and hard on the cane fields, the stubble still smoking, the fog billowing in white clouds off Bayou Teche. Lisa wants to walk inside the great pillows of white fog and stay there forever.

"I'm okay, Tookie. I'm ain't gonna use. I promise," she says.

"You know how you can tell when drunks and junkies are lying? Their lips are moving. Come to my house. I'll fix breakfast."

"I'm late for my appointment at the employment of-fice."

Tookie steps closer to her, her face suddenly feminine, tender, almost vulnerable. Her fingers rest on Lisa's fore-arm, her thumb caressing Lisa's skin for just a moment. "Herman will try to get you in the sack. But getting in your pants ain't what it's about. He wants you on the pipe and working his corner. I been there, Lisa. Herman Stanga is the devil."

Tookie forms a circle with her index finger and thumb around Lisa's wrist and squeezes, her mouth parting with her own undisguised need.

≈≈≈

Herman Stanga is full of rebop and snap-crackle-and-pop and knows how to put some boom-boom in your bam-bam, baby. Or at least that is his self-generated mystique as he cruises from place to place in New Iberia's old red-light district, a leather bag hanging from a strap on his shoulder, a pixie expression on his lean face, his mustache like a pair of tiny blackbird's wings against his gold skin.

His girls are called rock queens, although a lot of them have shifted gears and are doing crystal now because it burns off their fat and keeps them competitive on the street corner where they hook. Herman prefers them white, because there are black dudes who will always pay top dollar for white bread, no matter what kind of package it comes in. But, as he is fond of saying, he is "an Affirmative Action employer. Ain't nothing wrong with giving a country girl a crack at a downtown man."

Lisa did not lie to Tookie about her appointment at the state employment office. The problem was the three hundred people ahead of her when she arrived and the piano wire that someone is now tightening around her head with a wood peg. She lasts forty-five minutes in the waiting room, vomits in the bathroom, then drives down Railroad Avenue to the first liquor store she can find. The short-dog she buys may smell like a mixture of hair tonic and kerosene, but it goes down with a rush that is one notch south of the orgasmic moment she experienced when she first shot up with brown skag.

She finishes the bottle under the shade of a spreading oak by a small grocery store. Gangbangers with black kerchiefs tied down on their heads are taking turns at a weight set under the tree, curling the bar in to their bare chests, their steroid-swollen muscles almost popping out of their skin. Lisa screws the cap on the empty bottle and stares vacantly into space, then takes her time getting out of the car and dropping the bottle in a trash barrel. She has no reason to remain under a lichen-encrusted tree, in New Iberia's old brothel district, on a morning she should seek work, on a morning that somehow seems like a crossroads that has been set in her path. But the sun-spangled shade under the tree is a pleasant place to be, with her car door open to the wind, on a day that is both warm and cool at the same time, while the boys clank iron and leaves drift down on her windshield like gold coins.

She shuts her eyes and breathes the heavy odor of the fortified wine in and out of her lungs, and for just a moment, as though she is outside of her body, she sees Gerald kiss her cheek and place the flat of his hand on her belly.

Without invitation, a grinning man wearing a striped brown suit and an oxblood Stetson opens the passenger door and slides in beside her. He has two sweating cans of Budweiser balanced in his left palm and a fat package of warm boudin in the other. "Hey, darling, want to join me in a li'l snack?" he asks, already spreading the butcher paper open on the seat, filling the car with the delicious smell of ground sausage and spice and onions.

"I ain't here to score, Herman," she replies.

"I respect folks' choices. When they get clean, I say more power to them. But that don't mean I ain't their friend no more."

He peels the tab on one of the beer cans and lets the foam rise through the hole and well over the top and slide down the back of his hand. "Here you go, baby. Sip this while I cut you some boudin chunks. You found a job yet? All them evacuees is kind of messing up the labor market, ain't they?"

She is an evacuee, flooded out of the Lower Ninth Ward in Orleans Parish by Hurricane Katrina, shuttled from the Superdome to a shelter in New Iberia's City Park. In fact, she'd still be there or in a FEMA trailer camp if her aunt hadn't given her the use of the shotgun cabin in the Loreauville quarters. But Herman already knows that. Herman knows how to flatter, to indicate his listener is different, special, not part of a categorical group whose presence is starting to be resented and feared.

"That Budweiser is good and cold, ain't it?" he says. "Lookie here, drive me to my crib and let me make some calls. Can you do receptionist work, answer the phone, maybe seat people in a restaurant, stuff like that?"

"Sure, Herman."

"Then let's motivate on out of here, baby," he says, lifting his chin, indicating she should start the engine and drive the two of them to his Victorian home on Bayou Teche.

Herman acquired the house from a black physician who, for unknown reasons, signed over the deed and left town. No one ever knew where the physician or his family went, nor were they ever heard from again. The wood columns are eaten by termites, the ventilated green shutters askew on their hinges, the second-story rain gutters bleeding rust down the walls. The oak and pecan trees are so thick that sunlight never enters the house and no grass grows in the yard.

But Herman is not concerned with historical preservation. The swimming pool in his backyard is a glittering blue teardrop, coated with steam, where his girls float on inflated latex cushions, where bougainvillea drips as brightly as drops of blood on his latticework, where potted lime and Hong Kong orchid trees bloom year-round and assure his guests the season is eternal.

"Sit here and relax while I call in a couple of favors from some business associates," he says out on the terrace. "Have some of them veined shrimps. Ignore the ladies in the pool. They nice, but they ain't in your league, know what I mean? Hey, if I get you on in a hostess position, it's probably gonna be twelve or t'irteen dol'ars an hour. You all right wit' that?"

Lisa sits in the coolness of the sunshine and tries to concentrate on what she is doing. It's only noon and she has gone from the comfort of the fog at sunrise into the meeting at the church, then to the employment office and the liquor store and the shady oak tree where boys clanked iron and admired one another's bodies as though anatomical perfection were a stay against mortality. Now she is at the home of Herman Stanga, watching women she doesn't know swim in a sky-blue pool, while Herman paces back and forth behind the French doors, talking on the phone, undressing down to a thong, kicking his trousers in a rattle of change across the room.

The bayou is chocolate-brown, the sun a wobbling balloon of yellow flame trapped under its surface. The bayou conjures up images and memories she does not want to revisit. In her mind's eye she sees people wading in chest-deep water, the surface iridescent with a chemical sheen, fecal clouds rising from the bottom, a stench crawling into her nostrils that makes her gag. Then the knocking sound starts in her head and she has to press both fists against her temples to make it stop.

Why has she come to Herman's house? Does she really believe he wants to help her? What would Tookie say if she knew?

"I'm telling you, this is a nice lady, man," she hears Herman saying. "No, she ain't on welfare. No, she ain't got no personal problems or bad habits. What she got is my recommendation. Don't give me your trash, Rodney. I'm sending her over. You treat her right, nigger."

Herman clicks off the phone and slips on a robe that

hangs on his lithe frame like blue ice water. He motions Lisa inside and tells her to sit on a stool at a counter that separates the living room from the kitchen. "My cousin Rodney owns a couple of clubs in Lafayette and caters parties and banquets for rich people out at the Oil Center. All you got to do is supervise the buffet table and the punch bowl and make sure everybody getting the drinks they need. They want somebody know how to deal with the public. I told Rodney that's you, baby."

He's talking too fast for her. Her ears are popping and she thinks she hears voices yelling and the downdraft of helicopter blades. She realizes Herman is staring at her, his face disjointed. "You gonna get crazy on me?" he says.

"The Coast Guard helicopter took me off the roof. The blades was so loud nobody could hear. I was shouting and nobody could hear."

"Shouting what?" Herman asks. "What you talking about?"

"The Coast Guard man grabbed me around the chest and pulled me up on a cable. I couldn't t'ink. I could see trash and bodies in the water all the way to where the levee was broke. I cain't get that noise out of my head."

"What noise?"

"The knocking."

Herman brushes at a nostril with one knuckle and huffs air out his nose, his eyes flat, as though he's studying thoughts of a kind no one would ever guess at. He begins to massage the tendons in her shoulders. "You're tight as iron, Lisa. That ain't good for you. Come upstairs."

"No."

For just an instant, in the time it takes to blink, she sees the light in his eyes harden. Then he bites his lip softly and smiles to himself. "I respect you, darling. Wouldn't have our relationship no other way."

Now he's the pixie again, his tiny mustache flexing with his grin. He places a mirror on the corner, back side flat, and begins chopping up lines on it with a razor blade, shaping and sculpting each white row like an artwork. "I still got the best product in town. I don't force it on nobody. They hurting, need some medicine, I hep them out. But I ain't the captain of nobody else's soul."

"I don't want any, Herman," she says, the words catching like a wet bubble in her throat.

"If you can get by on a short-dog and a beer now and then, I say, 'Rock on, girl.' I say you a superwoman."

He removes a hundred-dollar bill from the pocket of his robe, rolls it into a crisp tube, and snorts a line up each nostril, the soles of his slippers slapping on the floor. He grabs his thonged phallus inside his open robe and pulls on it. "Tell me them coca leaves wasn't picked by Indian goddesses."

"I got to go, Herman," she says, because she is absolutely sure the knocking sound that has haunted her sleep and that sometimes comes aborning even in the midst of a conversation is about to begin again.

At the front door he presses the hundred-dollar bill into her palm and closes her fingers on it. "Get you some new threads. You fine-looking, Miss Lisa. Got the kind of class make a man's eye wander."

He lifts her hand, the one that holds the hundred-dollar bill, and kisses it. The cocaine residue on the paper seems to burn like a tiny ball of heat clenched inside her palm.

≈

The party she helps cater that night is held in a refurbished icehouse across the street from a Jewish cemetery shrouded by live oaks. It's raining outside, but the moon is full and visible through the clouds, and the shell parking lot is chained with rain puddles. A tin roof covers the old loading dock where years ago blocks of ice rushed down a chute into a wood box and once there were chopped into small pieces with ice picks by sweating black men. The roar of the rain on the tin roof is almost deafening and Lisa has a hard time concentrating on her work. She has another problem, too.

Rodney, the caterer, can't keep his hands off her. When he tells her how to arrange and freshen the salad bar, he keeps his palm in the middle of her back. When he walks her the length of the serving table, he drapes an arm over her shoulder. When she separates from him, he lets his fingers trail off her rump.

"Herman tole me you growed up here'bouts," he says, slipping his grasp around her triceps.

"My husband's daddy worked at this icehouse. He chopped up ice out there on the dock, in that wood box there," she replies.

He nods idly, as though processing her statement. "Your husband got killed in Iraq?"

She starts to answer, then realizes he isn't listening, that he's watching another worker pour a stainless-steel tray of okra gumbo into a warmer. His gaze breaks and his eyes come back on her. "Go ahead," he says.

"Go ahead what?"

"Say what you was saying."

"Can I get paid after work tonight? I got to hep my auntie wit' her mortgage."

"Don't see nothing wrong wit' that," he says.

He squeezes by her on his way to the kitchen, the thick outline of his phallus sliding across her rump.

The party becomes more raucous, grows in intensity, the males-only crowd emboldened by their numbers and insularity. Four bare-breasted women in spangled G-strings and spiked heels are dancing on a stage, fishnet patterns of light and shadow shifting across their skin. Outside, the rain continues to fall and Lisa can see the black-green wetness of the oak trees surrounding the Jewish cemetery, the canopy swishing against the sky, and she wonders if it is true that the unbaptized are locked out of heaven.

Why is she thinking such strange thoughts? She tries to think about her life in New Orleans before the hurricane, before Gerald's reserve unit was called up, before his Humvee was blown into scrap metal.

She had waited tables in a restaurant in Jackson Square, right across the street from the Café du Monde. There were jugglers and street musicians and unicyclists in the square, and crepe myrtle and banana trees grew along the piked fence where the sidewalk artists set up their easels. It was cool and breezy under the colonnades, and the courtyards and narrow passageways smelled of damp stone and spearmint and roses that bloomed in December. She liked to watch the people emerging from Mass at St. Louis Cathedral on Saturday evening and she liked bringing them the steaming trays of boiled crawfish, cob corn, and artichokes that were the restaurant's specialty. In fact, she loved New Orleans and she loved Gerald and she loved their one-story tin-roofed home in the Lower Ninth Ward.

But these thoughts cause her scalp to constrict and she thinks she hears hail bouncing off the loading dock outside.

"You got seizures or something?" Rodney asks.

"What?"

"You just dropped the ladle in the gumbo," he says.

She stares stupidly at the serving spoon sinking in the cauldron of okra and shrimp.

"Take a break," Rodney says.

She tries to argue, then relents and waits in a small office by the kitchen while Rodney gets another girl to fill in for her. He closes the door behind him and studies Lisa with a worried expression, then sits in a chair across from her and lights a joint. He takes a hit, holding it deep in his lungs, offering it to her while he lets out his breath in increments. Her hand seems to reach out as though it has a will of its own. She bends over and touches the joint to her lips and feels the wetness of his saliva mix with her own. She can hear the cigarette paper superheat and crinkle as she draws in on the smoke.

"I got to pay you off, baby."

" 'Cause I dropped the ladle?"

" 'Cause you was talking to yourself at the buffet table. 'Cause you in your own spaceship."

Someone outside twists the door handle and flings the door back on its hinges. Tookie Goula steps inside, the strap of her handbag wrapped around her wrist, her arms pumped. "You put that joint in your mout' again, I'm gonna break your arm, me. Then I'm gonna stuff this pimp here in a toilet bowl," she says.

Moments later, in Lisa's parked automobile, Tookie stares at Lisa with such intensity Lisa thinks she is about to hit her.

"Next time I'll let you drown," Tookie says.

Lisa looks at the Jewish cemetery and the oak trees thrashing against the sky and the rain puddles in the parking lot. The puddles are bladed with moonlight and she thinks of Communion wafers inside a pewter chalice, but she doesn't know why.

"What do you know about drowning, Tookie?"

Tookie seems to reflect upon Lisa's question, as though she, too, is bothered by the presumption and harshness in her own rhetoric. But the charitable impulse passes. "Get your head out of your ass. You want to fire me as your sponsor, do it now."

Lisa still has the hundred-dollar bill Herman Stanga gave her, plus the money she was paid by his cousin Rodney. She can score some rock or crystal or brown skag in North Lafayette and stay high or go on an alcoholic bender for at least two days. All she has to do is thank Tookie for her help and drive away.

"Where you think Limbo is at?" she says.

"What?"

"The place people go when they ain't baptized. Like all them Jews in that cemetery."

Tookie stares wanly at the parking lot, her face marked with a sad knowledge about the nature of loss and human inadequacy that she will probably never admit, even to herself.

≈≈≈

The next morning Lisa stands at the speaker's podium at the A.A. meeting in the Pentecostal church, her eyes fixed on the back wall, and owns up to drinking, using, and jerking her sponsor around. She says she intends to work the steps and to live by the principles of the program. Both the brevity of her statement and the sincerity in her voice surprise her. She receives a twenty-four-hour sobriety chip, then watches it passed around the room so each person at the meeting can hold it in his palm and say a silent prayer over it. She lowers her head to hide the wetness in her eyes.

"Eat breakfast wit' me. Up at the café," Tookie says.

"I'd like that," Lisa says.

"You gonna make it, you."

Lisa believes her. All the way to 3:00 p.m., when Herman Stanga pulls up to her shotgun house in the Loreauville quarters and kills his engine by her gallery. His car hood ticks like a broken watch.

"You ain't gonna unlatch the screen for me?" he says.

"I ain't got no reason to talk wit' you, Herman."

"Got me all wrong, baby. I done a li'l research on your financial situation. You should have gotten at least a hundred t'ousand dol'ars when your husband was killed. The gov'ment ain't paid you yet?"

She swallows and the tin rooftops and the narrow houses that are shaped like boxcars and the trees along the bayou go in and out of focus and shimmer in the winter sunlight.

"Gerald's divorce hadn't come t'rew yet," she says.

"What you mean?"

"His mama and his first wife was the beneficiaries on the policy. He didn't change the policy," she says, her eyes shifting off of Herman's, as though she were both confessing a sin and betraying Gerald.

Herman feeds a stick of gum into his mouth, smacks it in his jaw, and raises his eyebrows, as though trying to suppress his incredulity. "Tell me if I got this right. He's putting the blocks to you, but he goes off to Iraq and fixes it so you ain't gonna have no insurance money? That's the guy you moping around about?"

He begins to chew his gum more rapidly and doesn't wait for her to reply. "So what we gonna do about the eight-t'ousand-dol'ar tab you got? Also, what we gonna do about the twenty-t'ree hundred dol'ars you took out of Rodney's cashbox last night?"

"Cashbox?"

His head bounces up and down ironically, like it's connected to a rubber band. "Yeah, the cashbox, the one that was in the desk in the office where Rodney said to sit your neurotic ass down and wait for him. You t'ink you can rip off a man like Rodney and just do your nutcase routine and walk away?"

"I didn't steal no money. I don't owe you no eight t'ousand dol'ars, either."

" 'Cause you was so stoned out you got no memory of it." Then he begins to mimic her. " 'Tie me off, Herman. Give me just one balloon, Herman. I'll do anyt'ing, Herman. I'll be good to you, Herman. I'll pay you tomorrow, Herman.' "

How does he speak with such authority and confidence? Did she actually say those things? Is that who she really is?

"I ain't stole no money out of no office."

"Tell that to the sheriff when Rodney files charges. Open this goddamn door, bitch. You fixing to go on the installment plan."

She attacks his face with her nails and he hits her with his fist harder than she ever believed a human being could be hit.

≋

During the next six weeks Lisa comes to believe the person she thought was Lisa perhaps never existed. The new Lisa also learns that Hell is a place without geographical boundaries, that it can travel with an individual wherever she goes. She wakes to its presence at sunrise, aching and dehydrated, the sky like the watery, cherry-stained dregs in the bottom of a Collins glass. Whether picking up a brick of Afghan skunk in a Lafayette bus locker for Herman or tying off with one of his whores, sometimes using the same needle, Lisa moves from day into night without taking notice of clocks or calendars or the macabre transformation in the face that looks back at her from the mirror.

She attends meetings sometimes but either nods out or lies about the last time she drank or used. If pressed for the truth about where she has been or what she has done, she cannot objectively answer. Dreams and hallucinations and moments of heart-pounding clarity somehow meld together and become indistinguishable from one another. The irony is the knocking sound has finally stopped.

Sometimes Tookie Goula cooks for her, holds her hands, puts her in the shower when she is too sick to care for herself. Tookie has started to smoke again and some days looks haggard and hungover. At twilight on a spring evening they are in Lisa's bedroom and the live oaks along the bayou are dark green and pulsing with birds against a lavender sky. Lisa has not used or gotten drunk in the last twenty-four hours. But she thinks she smells alcohol on Tookie's breath.

"It's codeine. For my cough," Tookie says.

"It's a drug just the same," Lisa says. "You go back on the spike, you gonna die, Tookie."

Tookie lies down next to Lisa, then turns on her side and places one arm across Lisa's chest. Lisa doesn't resist but neither does she respond.

"You want to move in wit' me?" Tookie asks. "I'll hep you get away from Herman. Maybe we'll go to Houston or up Nort' somewhere, maybe open a café."

But Lisa is not listening. She rubs the balls of her fingers along one of the tattoos on Tookie's forearm.

"A mosquito bit me," Tookie says.

"No, you're back on the spike."

She kisses Tookie on the mouth and presses Tookie's head against her breast, something she has never done before. "You break my heart."

"You're wrong. I ain't used in t'ree years, me."

"Stop lying, stop lying, stop lying," Lisa says, holding Tookie tighter against her breast, as though her arms can squeeze the sickness out of both their bodies.

≋

It begins to rain and Lisa can smell fish spawning in the bayou and the odor of gas and wet leaves on the wind. She hears the blades of a helicopter thropping across the sky and sees lightning flicker on the tin roofs of her neighbors' homes. As she closes her eyes, she feels herself drifting upward from her bed, through the ceiling, into the coolness and freedom of the evening. The clouds form a huge dome

above her, like that of a cathedral, and she can see the vast-
ness of creation: the rain-drenched land, a distant storm
that looks like spun glass, a sea gone wine-dark with the setting of the sun.

Gerald loved me. We was gonna be married by a priest
soon as his divorce come through, she says to Tookie.

I know that, Tookie says.

Down there, that's where it happened.

What happened?

My sister was trying to hand up my l'il boy t'rew the
hole in the roof and they fell back in the water. I could hear
them knocking in there, but I couldn't get them out. My
baby never got baptized.

These t'ings ain't your fault, Lisa. Ain't nobody's fault.
That's what makes it hard. You ain't learned that, you?

Directly below, Lisa can see the submerged outline of
the house where she and her family used to live. The sun is
low on the western horizon now, dead-looking, like a piece
of tin that gives no warmth. Beneath the water's surface
Lisa can see tiny lights that remind her of broken Communion wafers inside a pewter chalice or perhaps the souls of
infants that have found one another and have been cupped
and given safe harbor by an enormous hand. For reasons
she cannot explain, that image and Tookie's presence bring
her a moment of solace she had not anticipated.

A Season

of Regret

Albert Hollister likes the heft of it, the coldness of the steel, the way his hand fits inside the lever action. Even though the Winchester is brand-new, just out of the box from Wal-Mart, he ticks a chain of tiny drops from a can of 3-in-One on all the moving parts, cocks and recocks the hammer, and rubs a clean rag over the metal and stock. The directions tell him to run a lubricated bore brush down the barrel, although the weapon has never been fired. After he does so, he slips a piece of white paper behind the chamber and squints down the muzzle with one eye. The oily spiral of light that spins at him through the rifling has an otherworldly quality about it.

He presses a half-dozen .30-30 shells into the tubular magazine with his thumb, then ejects them one by one on his bedspread. His wife has gone to town with the nurse's aide for her doctor's appointment and the house is quiet. The fir trees and ponderosa pine on the hillside are full of wind and a cloud of yellow dust rises off the canopy and sucks away over his barn and pasture. He picks up the shells and fits them back in the cartridge box, then puts the rifle and the shells in his closet, closes the door on them, and drinks a glass of iced tea on the front porch.

Down the canyon he can see the long roll of the Bitterroot Mountains, the moon still visible against the pale blueness of the sky, like a sliver of dry ice. He drains his glass and feels a terrible sense of fatigue and hopelessness wash through his body. If age brings wisdom, he has yet to see it in his own life. Across the driveway, in his north pasture, a large sorrel-colored hump lies in the bunchgrass. A pair of magpies descend on top of it, their beaks dipping into their bloody work. Albert looks at the scene with great sorrow on his face, gathers up a pick and a shovel from the garage, and walks down the hillside into the pasture. A yellow Labrador retriever bounds along behind him.

"Go back to the house, Buddy," Albert says.

The wind makes a sound like water when it sharks through the grass.

Albert had seen the bikers for the first time only last week. Three of them had ridden up the dirt road that splits his ranch in half, ignoring the PRIVATE ROAD sign nailed to the railed fence that encloses his lower pasture. They turned around when they hit the dead end two hundred yards north of Albert's barn, then cruised back through Albert's property toward the paved highway.

They were big men, the sleeves of their denim jackets scissored off at the armpits, their skin wrapped with tattoos. They sat their motorcycles as though they absorbed the throttled-down power of the engine through their thighs and forearms. The man in the lead had red hair and a wild beard and sweat rings under his arms. He seemed to nod when Albert lifted his hand in greeting.

Albert caught the tag number of the red-haired man's motorcycle and wrote it down on a scrap of paper that he put away in his wallet.

A half hour later he saw them again, this time in front of the grocery store in Lolo, the little service town two miles down the creek from his ranch. They had loaded up with canned goods and picnic supplies and sweating six-packs of beer and were stuffing them into the saddlebags on their motorcycles. He passed within three feet of them, close enough to smell the odor of leather, unwashed hair, engine grease, and woodsmoke in their clothes. One of them gargled with his beer before he swallowed it, then grinned broadly at Albert. He wore black glasses, as a welder might. Three blue teardrops were tattooed at the corner of his left eye.

"What's happening, old-timer?" he said.

"Not much outside of general societal decay, I'd say," Albert replied.

The biker gave him a look.

Five days later, Albert drove his truck to the Express Lube and took a walk down toward the intersection while he waited for his truck to be serviced. It was sunset and the sky was a chemical green, backdropped by the purple shapes of the Bitterroot Mountains. The day was cooling rapidly and Albert could smell the cold odor of the creek that wound under the highway. It was a fine evening, one augmented by families enjoying themselves at the Dairy Queen, blue-collar people eating in the Mexican restaurant, an eighteen-wheeler shifting down for the long pull over Lolo Pass. But the voices he heard on the periphery of his vision were like a dirty smudge on a perfect moment in time. The three bikers who had trespassed on his private road had blundered onto a young woman who had just gotten out of her car next to the town's only saloon.

Her car was a rust-eaten piece of junk, a piece of cardboard taped across the passenger window, the tires bald, a child's stuffed animal inside the back window. The woman had white-gold hair that was cut short like a boy's, tapered on the sides and shaved on the neck. Her hips looked narrow and hard inside her pressed jeans, her breasts firm against her tight-fitting T-shirt. She was trapped between her car and the three bikers, who behaved as though they had just run into an old friend and only wanted to offer her a beer. But it was obvious they were not moving, at least not without a token to take with them. A pinch on the butt or the inside of her thigh would probably do.

She lit a cigarette and blew the smoke at an upward angle, not responding, waiting for their energies to run down.

"How about a steak when you get off?" the man with the red beard asked.

"Sorry, I got to go home and wash out my old man's underwear," she said.

"Your old man, huh? Wonder why he didn't buy you a ring," the man with the beard replied. When he got no response, he tried again. "You a gymnast? 'Cause that's what you look like. Except for that beautiful pair of ta-tas, you're built like a man. That's meant as a compliment."

Don't mix in it. It's not your grief, Albert told himself.

"Hey, fellows," he said.

The bikers turned and looked at him, like men upon whom a flashbulb had just popped.

"I think she's late for work," Albert said.

"She sent you a kite on that?" the red-bearded man said, smiling.

Albert looked into space. "Y'all on your way to Sturgis?"

The third biker, who so far had not spoken, stuck an unfiltered cigarette into his mouth and lit it with a Zippo that flared on his face. His skin looked like dirty tallow in the evening light, his dark hair hanging in long strands on his cheeks. "She your daughter? Or your wife? Or your squeeze on the side?" he said. He studied Albert. "No, I can see that's probably not the case. Well, that means you should butt out. Maybe go buy yourself a tamale up at the café. A big, fat one, lot of juice running down it."

The bikers grinned into space simultaneously, as though the image conjured up shared meaning that only they understood.

Walk away, the voice inside Albert said.

"What's wrong with you fellows?" he asked.

"What?" the bearded man said.

"You have to bully a young woman to know who you are? What the hell is the matter with you?" Albert said.

The three bikers looked at one another, then laughed. "I remember where I saw you. On that ranch, up the creek a couple of miles. You walk up and down the road a lot, telling other people what to do?" the bearded man said.

The young woman dropped her cigarette to the ground and used the distraction to walk between the bikers, onto the wood porch of the saloon.

"Hey, come on back, sweet thing. You got a sore place, I'll kiss it and make it well," the biker with black glasses said.

She shot him the finger over her shoulder.

"Showtime is over," the bearded man said.

"No harm intended," Albert said.

"You got a church hereabouts?" the man with the black glasses said.

"There's a couple up the road," Albert said.

The three bikers looked at one another again, amused, shaking their heads.

"You're sure slow on the uptake," the bearded man said.

"If you go to one of those churches next Sunday, drop a little extra in the plate. Thank the Man Upstairs he's taking care of you. It's the right thing to do." He winked at Albert.

But the evening was not over. Fifteen minutes later, after Albert picked up his truck at the Express Lube, he passed by the saloon and saw the three men by the young woman's car. They had pulled the taped cardboard from the passenger-side window and opened the door. The biker with the beard stood with his feet spread, his thighs flexed, his enormous phallus cupped in his palm, urinating all over the dashboard and the seat.

Albert drove down the state highway toward the turnoff and the dirt road that led to his ranch. The hills were dark green against the sunset, the sharp outline of Lolo Peak capped with snow, the creek that paralleled the road sliding through shadows the trees made on the water's surface. He braked his truck, backed it around, and floored the accelerator, the gearshift vibrating in his palm. The note he left under the young woman's windshield wiper was simple: *The Idaho tag number of the red-haired man who vandalized your car is–* He copied onto the note the number he had placed in his wallet the day the bikers had driven through his property. Then he added: *I'm sorry you had this trouble. You did nothing to deserve it.*

He walked back toward his truck, wondering if the anonymity of his note was not a form of moral failure in itself. He returned to the woman's car and signed his name and added his phone number at the bottom.

On the way home the wind buffeted his truck, powdering the road with pine needles, fanning geysers of sparks out of a slash pile in a field. In the distance he saw a solitary bolt of lightning strike the ridgeline and quiver whitely against the sky. The air smelled of ozone and rain, but it brought him no relief from the sense of apprehension that seized his chest. There was a bitter taste in his mouth, like copper pennies, like blood, a taste that reminded him of his misspent youth.

It takes him most of the afternoon to hand-dig a hole in the pasture in order to bury the sorrel mare. The vinyl drawstring bag someone had wrapped over her head and cinched tight around her neck lies crumpled and streaked with ropes of dried saliva and mucus in the bunchgrass. The undersheriff, Joe Bim Higgins, watches Albert fling the dirt off the shovel blade onto the horse's flank and stomach and tail.

"I checked them out. You picked quite a threesome to get into it with," Joe Bim says.

"Wasn't of my choosing," Albert replies.

"Others might argue that."

Albert wipes the sweat off his forehead with the back of his forearm. The wind is up, channeling through the grass, bending the fir trees that dot the slopes of the hills that border both sides of his ranch. The sun is bright on the hills and the shadow of a hawk races across the pasture and breaks apart at the fence line. "Say again?"

"In the last year you filed a complaint because some kids fired bottle rockets on your property. You pissed off the developers trying to build a subdivision down on the creek. You called the president a draft-dodging moron in print. Some might say you have adversarial tendencies."

Albert thought about it. "Yes, I guess I do, Joe Bim. Particularly when a lawman stands beside my dead horse and tells me the problem is me, not the sonsofbitches who ran her heart out."

But Joe Bim is not a bad man. He removes a shovel from his departmental SUV and helps Albert bury the animal, wheezing down in his chest, his stomach hanging against his shirt like a water-filled balloon. "All three of those boys been in the pen," he says. "The one who hosed down the girl's car is a special piece of work. His child was taken away from him and his wife for its own protection."

Then Joe Bim tells Albert what the biker or his wife or both of them did to a four-month-old infant. Albert's eyes film. His clears his throat and spits into the grass. "Why aren't they in jail?" he says.

"Why do we have crack and meth in middle schools? The goddamn courts, that's why. But it ain't gonna change because you get into it with a bunch of psychopaths."

Albert packs down the dirt on top of his horse and lays a row of large, flat stones on top of the dirt. He cannot rid himself of the images Joe Bim's story has created in his mind. Joe Bim looks at him for a long time.

"How's the wife?" he asks.

"Parkinson's is Parkinson's. Some days are better than others," Albert says.

"You're a gentle man. Don't mess in stuff like this," Joe Bim says. "I'll get them out of town. They're con-wise. They know the hurt we can put on them."

You have no idea what you're talking about, Albert says to himself.

"What's that?" Joe Bim asks.

"Nothing. Thanks for coming out. Listen to that wind blow," Albert says.

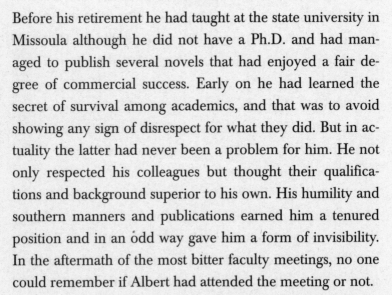

Before his retirement he had taught at the state university in Missoula although he did not have a Ph.D. and had managed to publish several novels that had enjoyed a fair degree of commercial success. Early on he had learned the secret of survival among academics, and that was to avoid showing any sign of disrespect for what they did. But in actuality the latter had never been a problem for him. He not only respected his colleagues but thought their qualifications and background superior to his own. His humility and southern manners and publications earned him a tenured position and in an odd way gave him a form of invisibility. In the aftermath of the most bitter faculty meetings, no one could remember if Albert had attended the meeting or not.

In truth, Albert's former colleagues, as well as his current friends, including Joe Bim Higgins, have no idea who he really is.

He never speaks of the road gang he served time on as a teenager, or the jails and oil-town flophouses he slept in from Mobile to Corpus Christi. In fact, he considers most of his youthful experience of little consequence.

Except for one event that forever shaped his thinking about the darkness that can live in the human breast.

It was the summer of 1955, and he had been sentenced to seven days in a parish prison after a bloody, nose-breaking brawl outside a bar on the Texas-Louisiana line. The male lockdown unit was an enormous iron tank, perforated with square holes, on the third floor of the building. Most of the inmates were check writers, drunks, wife beaters, and petty thieves. A handful of more serious criminals were awaiting transfer to the state prison farm at Angola. The inmates were let out of the tank at 7:00 a.m. each day and allowed the use of the bull run and the shower until 5:00 p.m., when they went back into lockdown until the next morning. By 6:00 p.m. the tank was sweltering, the smoke from cigarettes trapped against the iron ceiling, the toilets often clogged and reeking.

The treatment of the inmates was not deliberately cruel. The trusties ladled out black coffee, grits, sausage, and white bread for breakfast and spaghetti at noon. It was the kind of can where you did your time, stayed out of the shower when the wrong people were in there, never accepted favors from another inmate, and never, under any circumstances, sassed a hack. The seven days should have been a breeze. They weren't.

On Albert's fourth day, a trailer truck with two huge

generators boomed down on the bed, pulled to a stop with a hiss of air brakes, and parked behind the prison.

"What's that?" Albert asked.

"This is Lou'sana, boy. The executioner does it curbside, no extra charge," an inmate wiping his armpits with a ragged towel replied. His name was Deek. His skin was as white as a frog's belly and he was doing consecutive one-year sentences for auto theft and jailbreak.

But Albert was staring down from the barred window at a beanpole of a man on the sidewalk and was not concentrating on Deek's words. The man on the sidewalk was dressed western, complete with brim-coned hat, the bones of his shoulders almost piercing his snap-button shirt. He was supervising the unloading of a heavy rectangular object wrapped with canvas. "Say that again?" Albert said.

"They're fixing to fry that poor sonofabitch across the hall," Deek replied.

The clouds above the vast swampland to the west were the color of scorched iron, pulsing with electricity. Albert could smell an odor like dead fish on the wind.

"Some night for it, huh?" Deek said.

Without explanation, the jailer put the inmates into lockdown an hour early. The heat and collective stink inside the tank were almost unbearable. Albert thought he heard a man weeping across the hall. At 8:00 p.m. the generators on the truck trailer began to hum, building in velocity and force until the sounds of the street, the juke joint on the corner, and even the electric storm bursting above the swamp were absorbed inside a grinding roar that made Albert press his palms against his ears.

He would have sworn he saw lightning leap from the bars on the window, then the generators died and he could smell rain blowing through the window and hear a jukebox playing in a bar across the street from the jail.

The next morning, the jailer ran a weapons search on the tank and also sprayed it for lice. The inmates from the tank were moved into the hall and the room in which the condemned man had died. The door to the perforated two-bunk iron box in which he had spent his last night on earth was open, the electric chair already loaded on the trailer truck down below. When Albert touched the concrete surface of the windowsill he thought he could feel the residue from the rubber-coated power cables that had been stretched through the bars. He also smelled an odor that was like food that had fallen from a skillet into a fire.

Then he saw the man in the coned hat and western clothes emerge from a café across the street with a masculine-looking woman and two uniformed sheriff's deputies. They were laughing—perhaps at a joke or an incident that had just happened in the café. The man in the coned hat turned his face up into the light and seemed to look directly at Albert. His face was thin, the skin netted with lines, his eyes as bright and small as a serpent's.

"You waving at free people?" a guard said. He was a lean, sun-browned man who had been a mounted gunbull at Angola before he had become a sheriff's deputy and a guard at the parish prison. Even though the morning was still cool, his shirt was peppered with sweat, as though his body heat created its own environment.

"No, sir."

"So get away from the window."

"Yes, sir." Then he asked the question that rose from his chest into his mouth before he could undo the impulse. "Was that fellow crying last night?"

The guard lifted his chin, his mouth downturned at the corners. "It ain't none of your business what he was doing."

Albert nodded and didn't reply

"Food cart's inside now. Go eat your breakfast," the guard said.

"Don't know if I can handle any more grits, boss. Why don't you eat them for me?" Albert said.

The guard tightened the tuck of his shirt with his thumb, his expression thoughtful, his shoulders as square as a drill instructor's. He inhaled deeply through his nostrils. "Let's take a walk down to the second floor, get you a little better accommodated," he said. "Fine morning, don't you think?"

Albert never told anyone of what the guard did to him. But sometimes he smells the guard's stink in his sleep, a combination of chewing tobacco and hair oil and testosterone and dried sweat that had been ironed with starch into the clothes. In the dream he also sees the upturned face of the executioner, his skin lit in the sunshine, his friends grinning at a joke they had brought with them from the café. Albert has always wanted to believe this emblematic moment in his life was regional in origin, born out of ignorance and fear and redneck cruelty, perhaps one even precipitated by his own recklessness, but he knows otherwise.

Albert has learned that certain injuries go deep into the soul, like a stone bruise, and that time does not eradicate them. He knows that the simian creature that lived in the guard and the executioner took root many years ago in his own breast. He knows that, under the right circumstances, Albert Hollister is capable of deeds no one would associate with the professor who taught creative writing at the university and whose presence at faculty meetings was so innocuous it was not even remembered.

≈≈≈

To the east the fog is heavy and white and hangs in long strips on the hills bordering Albert's ranch. When the early sun climbs above the crest, it seems to burst among the trees like a shattered red diamond. From the kitchen window, where he is drinking coffee and looking down the long slope of his southern pasture, he sees a rust-eaten car coming up the road, its headlights glowing against the shadows that cover the valley floor. One headlight is out of alignment and glitters oddly, like the eye of a man who has been injured in a fight. The passenger window is encased with cardboard and silver duct tape.

The girl from the saloon knocks at his front door, dressed in colorless jeans and a navy-blue corduroy coat. She wears a cute cap and her cheeks are red in the wind. She is obviously awed by the size of his home, the massive amounts of quarried stone that support the two top floors, the huge logs that could probably absorb a cannon shell. Through the rear window of her vehicle, he can see a small boy strapped in a child's car seat.

"I wanted to tell you I'm sorry about what happened to your horse," she says.

"It's not your fault," Albert says.

Her eyes leave his, then come back again. He thinks he can smell an odor in her clothes and hair like damp leaves burning in the fall. He hears his wife call to him from the bedroom. "Come in," he tells the girl. "I have to see to Mrs. Hollister. She's been ill for some time now."

Then he wonders to himself why he has just told the girl his personal business.

"We're on our way to Idaho. I just wanted to thank you and to apologize."

"That's good of you. But it's not necessary."

She looks down the pasture at the frost on the barn roof and the wind blowing in the bunchgrass. She sucks in her cheeks, as though her mouth has gone dry. "They got your name from me, not from the undersheriff."

In the silence he can hear his wife getting up from the bed and walking toward the bathroom on her own. He feels torn between listening to the young woman and tending to his wife. "Run that by me again?" he says.

"One of them was my ex-husband's cellmate in Deer Lodge. They wanted to know your name and if it was you who called the cops. They're in the A.B. That's why I'm going to Idaho. I'm not pressing charges," she says.

"The Aryan Brotherhood?"

She sticks her hands in the pockets of her jacket and balls them into fists, all the time looking at the ground. Then Albert realizes she has not come to his home simply to apologize. He also realizes the smoke he smells on her clothes and person did not come from a pile of burning leaves.

"My boss is gonna send me a check in two weeks. At least that's what he says. My boyfriend is trying to get one of those FEMA construction jobs in New Orleans. But his P.O. won't give him permission to leave the state. I have enough money for gas to Idaho, Mr. Hollister, but I don't have enough for a motel."

"I see," he replies, and wonders how a man of his age could be so dumb. "Will fifty dollars help? Because that's all I have on me."

She seems to think about it. "That'd be all right," she says. She glances over her shoulder at the little boy strapped in the car seat. Her nails look bitten, the self-concern and design in her eyes undisguised. "The saloon will be open at ten."

"I don't follow you," he said.

"I could take a check. They'll cash it for me at the sa-loon."

He lets her words slide off his face without reacting to them. When he removes the bills from his wallet and places them in her hand, she cups his fingers in her palm. "You're a good man," she says.

"When are they coming?" he asks.

"Sir?"

He shakes his head to indicate he has disengaged from the conversation and closes the door, then walks down the hallway and helps his wife back to her bed. "Was that someone from the church?" she asks.

≈≈≈

During the night he hears hail on the roof, then high winds that make a rushing sound, like water, through the trees on the hillsides. He dreams about a place in South Texas where he and his father bobber-fished in a chain of ponds that had been formed by sheets of twisted steel spinning out of the sky like helicopter blades when Texas City exploded in February of 1947. In the dream, wind is blowing through a piney woods that borders a saltwater bay hammered with light. His father speaks to him inside the wind, but Albert cannot make out the words or decipher the meaning they contain.

In the distance he hears motorized vehicles grinding up a grade, throttling back, then accelerating again, working their way higher and higher up the mountainside, with the relentlessness of chain saws.

He wakes and sits up in bed, not because of the engines but because they have stopped—somewhere above his house, inside the trees, perhaps on the ridgeline where an old log road traverses the length of the canyon.

He removes the rifle from his closet and loads it. He disarms the security system and steps out onto the gallery, in the moonlight and the sparkle of frost on the bunchgrass. His hands and uncovered head and bare feet are cold. He levers a shell into the chamber but releases the hammer with his thumb so that it cannot drop by accident and strike the shell casing, discharging the round. The fir trees are black-green against the hillside, the arroyo behind his house empty. The air is clean and smells of pine and snow melting on the rocks and woodsmoke from a neighbor's chimney down the canyon. In the whisper of the wind through the trees he wants to believe the engine sounds in his dream are just that—the stuff of dreams. Far up the hill he hears a glass bottle break on stone and a motorcycle roar to life.

Inside the topmost trees three separate fires burst alight and fill the woods with shadows. The sound of motorcycle engines multiplies and three balls of flame move in different directions down the ridgeline. Inside the house, he calls 911 and through the back window he sees the silhouette of one rider towing a fireball that caroms off the undergrowth, the points of ignition fanning down the slope in the wind.

"What's the nature of your emergency?" the dispatcher asks.

"This is Albert Hollister, up Sleeman Gulch. At least three men on motorcycles are stringing fires down my ridgeline."

"Which way are they headed?"

"Who cares where they're headed? The wind is out of the southwest. I'll have sparks on my roof in a half hour. Get the goddamn pump trucks up here."

"Would you not swear, please?"

"These men are criminals. They're burning my land."

"Repeat, please. I cannot understand what you're saying."

His voice has wakened and frightened his wife. He comforts her in her bed, then goes outside again and watches a red glow spread across the top of the valley. The summer has been dry and the fire ripples through the soft patina of grass at the base of the trees and superheats the air trapped under the canopy. A sudden rush of cold wind through the timber hits the fire like an influx of pure oxygen. Flame balloons out of the canopy and in seconds turns fir trees into black scorches dripping with sparks. He can hear deer running across rocks and see hundreds of bats flying in and out of a sulfurous yellow cloud that has formed above the flames. He connects a hose to the faucet on the back of the house and sprays the bib of green grass on the slope, his heart racing, his mouth dry with fear.

≈

By noon the next day the wind has died and inside the smell of ash is another odor, one that reminds him of the small room on the third floor of the parish prison where a man was strapped down in a wood chair and cooked to death with thousands of volts of electricity. Joe Bim Higgins stands next to Albert in the south pasture and stares up the hillside at the burned rocks and great stands of fir that are now rust-colored, as though stricken by blight.

Joe Bim blows his nose into a handkerchief and spits into the grass. "We found a sow and her cub inside a dead-fall. The fire was probably crowning when they tried to outrun it," he says.

"Where are they, Joe Bim?" Albert asks.

"Just up there where you see that outcropping." He tries to pretend his misunderstanding of Albert's question is sincere, then gives it up. "I had all three of them in a holding cell at seven this morning. But they got an alibi. Two people at their campground say they was at the campground all night."

"You cut them loose?"

Joe Bim is not a weak man or one who has avoided paying dues. He was at Heartbreak Ridge and one side of his face is still marbled from the heat flash of a phosphorous shell that exploded ten feet from his foxhole. "I can't chain-drag these guys down the Blackfoot highway because you don't like them. Look, I've got two deputies assigned to watch them. One of them throws a cigarette butt on the sidewalk—"

"Go back to town," Albert says.

"Maybe you don't know who your real friends are."

"Yeah, my wife and my yellow Lab, Buddy. I'd include my sorrel, except the two of us buried her."

"You're like me, Albert. You're an old man and you can't accept the fact you can't have your way with everything. Grow up and stop making life hard for yourself and others."

Albert walks away without replying. Later, he spreads

lime on the carcasses of the bears that died in the fire and tries not to think the thoughts he is thinking.

≈≈≈

That night, during a raging electric storm, Albert leaves his wife in the care of the nurse's aide and drives in his pickup to the only twenty-four-hour public campground on the Blackfoot River in Missoula County, his lever-action rifle jittering in the rack behind his head. It's not hard to find the three bikers. Their sky-blue polyethylene tent is huge, brightly lit from the inside, the extension flaps propped up on poles to shelter their motorcycles. Lightning flickers on the hillside across the river, limning the trees, turning the current in the river an even deeper black. The smell of ozone in the air makes Albert think of the Gulf Coast and his youth and the way rain smelled when it blew across the wetlands in the fall. He thinks of his father, who died while returning from a duck-hunting camp in Anahuac, Texas, leaving Albert to fend for himself. He wonders if this is the way dementia and death eventually steal upon a man's soul.

Down the road he parks his truck inside a grove of Douglas fir trees that are shaggy with moss and climbs up the hill into boulders that look like the shells of giant gray turtles. He works his way across the slope until he can look down upon the bikers' campsite. In the background the river is like black satin, the canyon roaring with the sounds of high water and reverberated thunder. The flap of the bik-

ers' tent is open and Albert can see three men inside, eating
from GI mess kits, a bottle of stoppered booze resting
against a rolled sleeping bag. They look like workingmen
on a summer vacation, enjoying a meal together, perhaps
talking about the fish they caught that day. But Albert
knows their present circumstances and appearance and behavior have nothing to do with who they really are.

They could as easily wear starched uniforms as they do
jailhouse tats. Their identity lies in their misogyny and violence and cruelty to animals and children, not the blue
teardrops at the corner of the eyes or the greasy jeans or the
fog of testosterone and dried beer sweat on their bodies.
These are the same men who operated Robespierre's tor-
ture chambers. They're the burners of the Alexandrian Library, the brownshirts who pumped chlorine gas into
shower rooms. They use religions and flags that allow them
to peel civilizations off the face of the earth. There is no difference, Albert tells himself, between these men and a
screw in a parish prison on the Louisiana-Texas border
where a guard frog-walked a kid in cuffs down to an isola-
tion area, shoved him to his knees, and closed the door on
the outside world.

The rain looks like spun glass blowing in front of the
open tent flap. The biker with the red beard emerges from
the opening, fills his lungs with air, and checks his motorcycle. He wipes off the frame and handlebars with a clean rag
and admires the perfection of his machine. Albert levers a
round into the chamber and steadies his rifle across the top
of a large rock. The notch of the steel sight moves across

the man's mouth and throat, the broad expanse of his chest, the hair blossoming from his shirt, then down his stomach and scrotum and jeans that are stiff with road grime and engine grease and glandular fluids.

In his mind's eye Albert sees all the years of his youth reduced to typewritten lines written on a sheet of low-grade paper. He sees the paper consumed by a white-hot light that burns a hole through the pulp, curling through the typed words, releasing images that he thought he had dealt with years ago but in reality has not. In the smoke and flame he sees a stretch of rain-swept black road and his father's car embedded under the frame of a tractor-trailer rig; he sees the naked, hair-covered thighs of a former Angola gunbull looming above him; he sees the ax-bladed face of a state executioner, a toothpick in his mouth, his eyes staring whimsically at Albert, as though it is Albert who is out of sync with the world and not the man who cinches the leather straps tightly to the wrists and calves of the condemned. Albert raises the rifle sight to the red-bearded man's chest and, just as a bolt of lightning splits a towering ponderosa pine in half, he squeezes the trigger.

The rifle barrel flares into the darkness and he already imagines the bullet on its way to the red-bearded man's chest. The round is copper-jacketed, soft-nosed, and when it strikes the man's sternum, it will flatten and topple slightly and core through the lungs and leave an exit wound the size of Albert's thumb.

My God, what has he done?

Albert stands up from behind the boulder and stares

down the hillside. The bearded man has taken a candy bar from his pocket and is eating it while he watches the rain blowing in the light from the tent flap.

He missed, thanks either to the Lord or to the constriction in his chest that caused his hand to jerk or maybe just to the fact he's not cut out of the same cloth as the man he has tried to kill.

Albert grasps the rifle by the barrel and swings it against a boulder and sees the butt plate and screws burst loose from the stock. He swings the rifle again, harder, and still breaks nothing of consequence loose from either the wood or the steel frame. He flings the rifle like a pinwheel into the darkness, the sight on the barrel's tip ripping the heel of his hand.

He cannot believe what happens next. The rifle bounces muzzle-down off the roof of a passing SUV, arcing back into the air with new life, and lands right in front of the bikers' tent.

He drives farther down the dirt road, away from the bikers' camp, his headlights off, rocks skidding from his tires into the canyon below.

When he gets back home, he strips off his wet clothes and sits in the bottom of the shower stall until he drains all the hot water out of the tank. His hands will not stop shaking.

〰〰

The rains are heavy the following spring and in May the bunchgrass in Albert's pastures is tall and green, as thick as

Kansas wheat, and the hillsides are sprinkled with wildflowers. In the evening whitetail and mule deer drift out of the
trees and graze along the edge of the irrigation canal he has
dug from a spring at the base of the burned area behind his
house. He would like to tell himself that the land will con-
tinue to mend, that a good man has nothing to fear from
the world and that he has put aside the evil done to him by
the bikers. But he has finally learned that lying to oneself is
an offense for which human beings seldom grant themselves absolution.

He comes to believe that acceptance of a wintry place
in the soul and a refusal to speak about it to others is as
much consolation as a man gets, and for some odd reason
that thought seems to bring him peace. He is thinking these
thoughts as he returns home from his wife's funeral in June.
Joe Bim Higgins is sitting on the front steps of his gallery,
the trousers of his dress suit stuffed inside his cowboy boots,
a Stetson hat balanced on his knee, a cigarette almost
burned down to a hot stub between two fingers. A pall-
bearer's ribbon is still in his lapel.

"The old woman wants me to invite you to dinner
tonight," Joe Bim says.

"I appreciate it," Albert replies.

"You never heard no more from those bikers, huh?"

"Why would I?"

Joe Bim pinches out the end of his cigarette, field-strips
the paper, and watches the tobacco blow away in the wind.
"Got a call two days ago from Sand Point. The one with the

red beard killed the other two, and an Indian woman for good measure. The three of them was drunk and fighting over the woman."

"I'm not interested."

"The killing got done with an 1894-model Winchester. Guess who it's registered to? How'd they end up with your rifle, Albert?"

"Maybe they found it somewhere."

"I think they stole it out of your house and you didn't know about it. That's why you didn't report it stolen." Joe Bim folds his hands and gazes at the hillside across the road and the wildflowers ruffling in the wind.

"They killed an innocent person with it?" Albert asks.

"If she was hanging with that bunch, she bought her own ticket. Show some humility for a change. You didn't invent original sin."

Albert starts to tell Joe Bim all of it—the attempt he made on the biker's life, the deed the sheriff's deputy had done to him when he was eighteen, the accidental death of his father, the incipient rage that has lived in his breast all his adult life—but the words break apart in his throat before he can speak them. In the silence he can hear the wind coursing through the trees and grass, just like the sound of rushing water, and he wonders if it is blowing through the canyon where he lives or through his own soul. He wonders if his reticence with Joe Bim is not indeed the moment of absolution that has always eluded him. He waits for Joe Bim to speak again but realizes his friend's crooked smile is one of puzzlement, not omniscience, that the puckered skin on the side of his face is a reminder that the good people of the world each carry their own burden.

Albert feeds his dog and says a prayer for his wife. Then he drives down the dirt road with Joe Bim in a sunset that makes him think of gold pollen floating above the fields.

The
Molester

He told all the kids to call him Frank. He had married into oil money, in this case a stone-deaf woman in the old Memorial District out by Rice University. When she died, Frank moved into a bachelor apartment with a swimming pool not far from the city park where Nick Hauser and I hung out during the summer of 1949. Frank drove a metallic-green Chevy convertible with a white top, rolled leather seats, and a polished walnut dashboard. In the late afternoon he would park it under shade trees and watch the kids playing on the softball diamond or working out on the chained-up sets of iron weights and the heavy bag in the lee of the park house.

Sometimes a bag of golf clubs was propped up in the backseat of Frank's car. He was a hard-bodied, athletic man, perhaps forty, his skin sun-browned, his thinning black hair combed straight back on his head. He smoked gold-tipped cigarettes and lit them with a tiny leather-encased lighter. One time he showed the lighter to me and Mary Jo Scarlotti and two other girls; the girls' shorts were rolled up high on their thighs, almost to their rumps. When the lighter was passed to me, Frank took it out of my hand and gave it to Mary Jo.

"I got that off a Jap colonel at Saipan," he said.

"Did you kill him, Frank?" one of the other girls asked, her mouth turned up at the corner.

"Not me. I was in Intelligence," he said, and winked behind his sunglasses.

Then he took the two other girls for a drive and left Mary Jo and me at the curb. "I'm glad you didn't go with him," I said.

Mary Jo had bongos that made my windpipe close up when I looked at them too long. "I think he's nice," she said.

The next day a new director showed up at the park house. Her name was Terry Anne and she was a magician at Ping-Pong, volleyball, and every kind of handicraft. She had thick, chestnut-colored hair and didn't have to wear makeup to be pretty. She wore jeans and tennis shoes to work and smelled like strawberry shampoo when her office heated up in the afternoon. I found every excuse to go into Terry Anne's office.

The first time she saw Frank unloading three junior high girls at the curb, she headed straight across the grass for his car. We could see her raise her finger in his face, her back stiff with anger, her mouth moving rapidly. Then she strode back to the park house, glancing back over her shoulder to ensure Frank was gone.

The next afternoon I saw Frank smoking a cigarette in the hot shade of the trees, not far from where Nick was laying it into the heavy bag. "Where's Terry Anne?" he asked.

"Inside the park house," I replied.

"You saw her yelling at me yesterday?"

I shrugged, my eyes downcast.

"Your name is Charlie, isn't it?" he said. He smiled at the corner of his mouth.

"Yes, sir."

"I'm not a 'sir.' Listen, Charlie. Terry Anne's a dyke. I tried to turn her around but didn't have any success, know what I mean? That's why she's got it in for me. What's your friend's name, the guy on the bag?"

"Nick," I said.

"Tell him to get up on the balls of his feet. Your jab's no good unless your weight is already forward. You box?" he said.

"A little. I had rheumatic fever in first grade."

He flicked his cigarette away and combed his hair, his eyes on Nick.

Later, I told Nick what Frank had said about getting up on the balls of his feet.

"He ought to know what he's talking about. He's a sponsor for the Golden Gloves," Nick said.

"What's a dyke?" I said.

"A guy with a male and a female organ. At least I think," Nick replied.

"Stay away from that guy," I said.

"You worry too much," Nick said. He grinned from ear to ear, his dun-colored crew cut spiked with sweat, his throat beaded with dirt rings.

Nick wasn't afraid of anything.

≈≈≈

The park was an island, a neutral ground, sandwiched between a respectable neighborhood of one-story tree-shaded brick homes and, three blocks away, another neighborhood where the houses were wood-frame and peeling, the yards bare, the early sun like a dust-veiled egg yolk. My mother and I lived in the neighborhood of bare yards. Our neighbors took pride in their lack of schooling, raised their children as livestock, and shot stray cats or dogs with BB guns. After I threw my morning paper route, I always headed straight for the park.

The park contained not only a baseball diamond and elevated plank seats shaded by live oak trees, but also a fountain and cement wading pool, tetherball poles, picnic tables and barbecue pits. The Popsicle truck arrived daily at 3:00 p.m., ringing with music, and on Monday nights there was a free outdoor movie.

For Nick and me, the park's green borders had been the edges of Eden, and no evil should have been able to penetrate them. But I heard stories about events that took place in the park after the field lights had blackened and cooled, when Negroes or Mexicans came into the park to fight white kids with chains, switchblades, and sometimes zip guns. One morning I saw Terry Anne on her knees, trying to scrub a horsetail of tiny red dots off the stucco wall of the park house with bleach and soap.

"What's that, Terry Anne?" I asked.

"Don't you or Nick hang around here after the park closes," she said. There was anger and recrimination in her voice.

"We don't," I replied.

She dropped her scrub brush in a bucket. A gray bar of industrial-strength Lava soap churned to the surface. Her face was hot when she looked up at me. "I saw Nick get in Frank Wallace's car yesterday. I want both you boys in my office before noon," she said.

"Why are you so mad?" I said.

But she resumed scrubbing the wall, working the bristles hard into the stucco, her jaw as tight as a drumhead.

Three hours later, in her office, she read us the riot act. Nick listened passively, his eyes looking innocently upward at the walls, the ceiling, the top shelves where Terry Anne kept all her board games and leather-craft tools. "Are you hearing me?" she said.

"I'm gonna fight in the Gloves. I'm gonna fight Angel Morales," Nick said.

"Angel Morales will kill you," Terry Anne said.

"I can kick Angel's butt. Frank says I can," Nick replied.

Terry Anne's mouth was pinched, her face without color, her hands balled into fists on top of her desk blotter. "Frank Wallace does nothing for anyone unless there's something in it for Frank Wallace. But maybe you'll have to find that out on your own," she said.

"What does it mean 'to turn somebody around'?" I asked.

"*What?* What did you say?" she said.

Outside, Nick punched me on the arm. "Are you crazy? Why'd you ask her that?" he said.

"Frank said he tried to turn her around. I didn't know what that meant," I replied.

"You do now." Then he shook his head and grinned. "You're an innocent guy, Charlie. That's why I'm always gonna look out for you."

"Why'd you go off with Frank?"

"I'm gonna be in the Gloves. Frank is Frank. What's the big deal? Give it a time-out, will you?" he replied.

Angel Morales's father was a janitor at the Catholic elementary I had attended. Angel used to ride to work with his father on the bus, his lunch folded inside a paper bag that seemed to always have a grease stain on it. His hair was jet-black, except for a white patch in it that had been caused by malnutrition. He never joined in our games at recess, never spoke in class unless called upon, and never let racial remarks made behind his back register in his face. In seventh grade, Angel and three other Mexican boys robbed a grocery store and shot the owner. Angel spent the next year three years in the Texas State Reformatory.

When he came out, he wore a pachuco cross tattooed on the back of each thumb and a purple heart inside his right forearm. Some said the purple heart was to hide the needle tracks from the dope he shot in his veins. But anyone who'd ever put on the gloves with Angel knew he was no junkie. His right cross split lips; his left jab could drive an unprotected eye into the skull. He wasn't a bad kid; he just didn't take prisoners.

On Saturday afternoon I paid for Mary Jo Scarlotti's ticket at the Alabama Theater. In the darkness I placed my hand on top of her left wrist. Her gaze was fastened on the screen and she showed no indication whether she approved or disapproved of my holding her hand. Then I saw her eyes follow a silhouette crossing the space between the screen and front row of seats, a silhouette that was eating popcorn, the shoulders bent in a question-mark posture, the way hoods walked on the north side of town. She took her hand from under mine and turned her head slightly so she could watch the figure walk up the aisle.

"That's Angel Morales," I said.

"A Mexican has the right to go to the movies, too," she said.

"I didn't say he didn't," I replied.

"I'm gonna get some popcorn. You got fifteen cents?" she said.

Her rump brushed in my face as she worked her way out to the aisle.

≋

Early Sunday morning I was throwing my paper route up on Waugh Drive when I saw Angel Morales in a jalopy full of Mexican teenagers. They pulled in to a closed filling station on the corner and went to work on the cold-drink machine, slipping the iron dispenser lock with a coat hanger so they could slide the soda bottles out one at a time without paying. The street was totally deserted, the softness of the morning tinged with the smell of garbage in the alleyways.

Angel lit a cigarette on the corner, blew smoke at an upward angle, and gestured for me to stop my bike. He wore a short-sleeve maroon shirt unbuttoned on his chest, the collar turned up on his neck, and pointed black shoes we used to call "stomps," his hair cut short, faintly iridescent with oil.

"Want a soda?" he asked.

"No, thanks."

"Your buddy Nick is telling people he's gonna rip my ass."

"Maybe he might do it," I replied, and instantly regretted my words.

But Angel only grinned and looked away from me. Then his eyes came back on mine, his mouth still grinning. "You're stand-up, Charlie. Sure you don't want a soda?" he said.

"No."

"Tell Nick I'm sorry I got to hurt him. But that's the way it is. That was you with Mary Jo Scarlotti at the show yesterday?"

"Maybe."

"I hear she's hot to trot."

"Screw you, Angel."

"Don't push your luck," he said.

Nick's father was a dutiful religious man and firm disciplinarian from a family of boxers in Mobile. He had given Nick a set of sixteen-ounce Everlast gloves when Nick was only ten, but he worked a six-day week at a laundry service to make an austere livelihood for his wife and three children, and he was often too tired to spend a great deal of time with Nick. So our park director, Terry Anne, became Nick's coach and I was the cut man, even though I could not forget the fact Nick had gone off with Frank one day and perhaps had made a deal with the devil.

When the afternoon began to cool and shadows grew across the baseball diamond, Terry Anne unfolded a metal chair among the weight sets and instructed Nick while he smacked the heavy bag, rattling it on its chain, sweat flicking off his hair against the leather.

"No, no, no, close it up, chin tucked in, head down," she said, rising from her chair, holding the bag steady. "If he gets you in a clench, he'll head-butt you and thumb you in the eye. When you're under his guard, you whack him just below the heart. Then you whack him again. You hook him so hard you make him spit blood on you."

"How did you learn all this, Terry Anne?" I said.

"You know who Lefty Felix Baker is?" she asked.

"The best boxer in Houston," I said.

"He didn't learn to fight at First Baptist," she said.

I'm sure her statement made sense to someone older than I, but Terry Anne was a beautiful riddle, and who was I to require that she make sense or be more than the mentor she was. After Nick had worn himself out on the bag, she draped a towel over his shoulders, then, as an afterthought, blotted the sweat out of his eyes with it. "You know, you might just surprise a lot of folks," she said.

That summer was marked by both drought and sudden electrical storms over the Gulf, an unexpected infusion of cold air into the park during a ball game, a burst of rain-flecked wind gusting plumes of dust high in the air. It was also the summer that we heard the Russians had developed the atom bomb. While the night sky pulsed with lightning that made no sound, World War II vets, wearing Hawaiian shirts, drank iced-down bottles of Jax and Pearl beer in the stands and talked about nuclear war. They talked about cities that would be melted into green glass. I wanted to stop my ears.

Mary Jo Scarlotti had taken to wearing shorts with lace sewn on the hems, and a gold chain and cross that hung inside her cleavage. She tied her shirt under her breasts when she played volleyball and danced up and down after spiking the ball into an opponent's face. On the Fourth of July she climbed up in a tree to put a bird back in its nest, then plummeted ten feet, her arms outspread, as though she had been crucified on the air, knocking all the wind out of her.

I tried to shake her awake and not look at the torn button on the top of her shirt. Suddenly her eyes clicked open, like a doll's.

"I thought you were dead," I said.

"Of course not. Here, listen to my heart," she said.

"What?"

"Silly," she said, and pressed the side of my head against her breast.

She stroked my hair while I listened to the whirring sounds inside her chest. Her perspiration smelled like talcum powder and flowers. Out of the corner of my vision, I saw a kid lift a yellow baseball bat in front of him and smack a ball across the grass.

The next afternoon I bought Mary Jo a banana split at the ice cream store next to the old fire station on Westheimer. We walked back toward the park to play Ping-Pong, then Frank's convertible pulled alongside us, the dual Hollywood mufflers throbbing softly against the asphalt, the steel curb feelers on his fenders scraping against the concrete. Angel Morales sat in the passenger seat, hunched forward, grinning at nothing, a deck of Luckies folded in the sleeve of his T-shirt.

"Hop in. I'm barbecuing by the pool," Frank said.

"We're going to the park," I replied.

"I'm hungry. I didn't get to eat supper," Mary Jo said.

Frank opened the door for her. She squeezed behind him into the backseat, the tops of her breasts bulging out of her shirt. "I got a swimsuit just your size," he said to her.

I watched them drive down a long street that was flanged on each side by trees and clipped lawns of St. Augustine grass and brick houses that had turned mauve-colored in the sunset. Mary Jo turned and looked back at me, her face like a white balloon. Then she was gone.

I went back to the park to find Nick, but he had left for home. I got on my bicycle, one with fat tires and canvas saddlebags inset in wood racks above the rear fender, and rode to Frank's apartment complex. I could smell meat cooking on a grill and hear water splashing and Frank and Mary Jo's voices on the other side of a brick wall.

I climbed a side stairs onto a second-story walkway that overlooked the shallow end of the pool. Frank was showing Mary Jo how to swim on her back. One hand was propped under the nape of her neck, the other moving back and forth from the bottom of her spine to the backs of her thighs, as though only his touch could keep her from sinking. The underwater lights were on, and her hair floated out from her head like black ink while she giggled and spit water from her mouth.

Behind me, I heard a hiss of released carbonation as someone sank a beer opener into a can.

"I think he's AC/DC, so Mary Jo's not necessarily in danger," Angel Morales said.

He upended a can of Grand Prize and looked at me over the bottom as he drank. He wore a pair of yellow swim trunks that stuck wetly to his genitalia and there was a smear of salt on his mouth from the top of the beer can.

"What's AC/DC?" I asked.

"It means don't take a leak next to Frank at a public urinal," he answered. "What are you doing here, Charlie?"

I started to answer, then realized I didn't know why I was there. At first I thought my concern was for Mary Jo. Or at least for Nick. But that wasn't it. "Frank doesn't have any business at the park. It's for kids. It's supposed to be safe," I said.

"Check it out after midnight and tell me about it," Angel replied.

"You let Frank use you for bait, Angel."

Angel's eyes were lustrous, like obsidian, unfocused, his thoughts buried deep in his face. He pawed at his cheek with four fingers and balanced his beer can on the railing. Down below, Mary Jo dipped under the water and swam like a giant fish past Frank's legs. Angel stepped close to my face, his breath touching my mouth.

"Wake up, Charlie," he said. "Mary Jo Scarlotti's family runs whorehouses in Galveston. That park director broad, what's her name, Terry Anne, was Frank's pump. You don't get no free lunch in this world. Now beat it."

≈≈≈

The next morning I spaded out my mother's flower bed and didn't go to the park. At noon Nick came to the house, his baseball glove hooked by its strap through his belt. The sun was white in the sky, the air like a moist cotton glove on the skin, the street blown with dust. The grass in our yard was yellow and there wasn't a teaspoon of shade on it.

"You punished or something?" he said.

"Not really," I said, pushing the shovel deep into the soil next to the house's foundation.

"The fight's Saturday morning. You're gonna be there, right?"

"Did Frank do something to you, Nick?"

It was quiet a long time. "You trying to hurt me?" he asked.

"Is it true?"

"I'm gonna hose Angel Morales in the first round. Then I'm gonna get a shot at the Regionals. But you don't need to be there, Charlie. Not Saturday, not ever," he said.

He walked down the street, peeling off his shirt, popping the dust off it like a whip, his ball glove flopping on his hip.

≈≈≈

Because I lived closer to the park than Nick, Terry Anne had told me to meet her there at 8:00 a.m. Saturday, then we would pick up Nick in her car and drive to the gym on the north side of town. But even though I woke that morning at first light, I found ways not to look at clocks, so that 8:00 a.m. would come and go without my making a deliberate choice to abandon my best friend.

But by eight-thirty I couldn't take it any longer. I hurried to the park, only to discover Terry Anne had gone. In her supply closet I found the bucket she had used to scrub blood from a gang fight off the wall of the park house, the bar of Lava soap glued to the bottom, the tin sides crusty from evaporated bleach water. I gathered up a roll of adhesive tape, a box of cotton swabs, a bottle of iodine and one of rubbing alcohol, and, along with two clean towels, put them in the bucket. Then I filled a water bottle from the tap, corked it, and caught the bus on Westheimer.

Downtown I transferred to another bus that took me into a neighborhood of auto repair shops, vacant lots piled with construction debris, vandalized filling stations, and nineteenth-century frame houses whose tin roofs shimmered in the heat.

The gym's windows were layered with white paint, the name of a tire company still faintly legible on one wall.

When I opened the door I saw a boxing ring inside a cavernous stone room, the folding chairs filled with people who did not look like fans at a Golden Gloves event.

"Where you going, bub?" a man at the door said. He wore a white shirt and slacks, and his body was shaped like a huge, upended football.

"I'm working Nick Hauser's corner," I said.

"That your spit bucket?" he said.

"Sure. Plus my medical supplies. I'm the cut man," I replied.

He smiled at another man, then looked back at me. "Better get on it, cut man. Him and Angel Morales are up next," he said.

The room stank of cigars, shower mold, hair oil, and sweaty workout clothes. A blackboard on one wall gave odds on the fighters, and a bone-white man in a fedora, strap undershirt, and tightly belted zoot slacks was taking bets at a plank bar. His arms and shoulders were streaked with body hair, his mouth formed meditatively into a cone when he wrote a wager on a notepad and tore a slip off for the bettor.

Two fighters, both about seventeen, neither wearing headgear, climbed from the ring and walked down the hallway to the dressing room. One of them had a bloody nose and an eye that had become a knot the size of a duck's egg. I saw Terry Anne in a folding chair by ringside, biting the corner of her lip, constantly twisting her head to see if Nick had come out of the dressing room. Then she saw me walking toward her, and I could tell by the way she looked past me at the front door, she was hoping Nick's father was with me.

"Why weren't you at the park house? You made us late," she said.

"Nick didn't want me," I replied.

"You could fool me," she said.

I knew she was taking her frustration and anger out on me because she had nowhere else to put it, but I didn't hold it against her. She was the only woman in the room, and the men sitting around us made me think of piranhas nudging their snouts against the wall of a fish tank.

"This isn't the Gloves, is it?" I said.

"Go down to the corner pay phone and call Nick's house. You tell his mother her son has impacted shit between his ears and she'd better get ahold of his father at work." She took a nickel from her purse and pressed it into my palm. "Do what I say, Charlie."

"Nick would never forgive either one of us," I replied.

She blew out her breath and gave it up. She had put on makeup and earrings and looked strangely beautiful inside the grayness of the gym, as though she were the only person there possessed of flesh tones and a red mouth and hair that was natural and full of tiny lights. Then I saw her throat swallow, and I realized how someone even as brave and decent as Terry Anne had her limits and didn't always do well when confronted with forces that sometimes are simply too much for us.

"Nick's not afraid. We shouldn't be, either, Terry Anne," I said.

"They're going to use Nick for shark meat. Now shut up, Charlie," she replied.

She was right. Frank Wallace had been sitting in the back of the room with three men who looked like gangsters. When Nick and Angel came out of the dressing room, he got up from his chair like he was going to greet both of them. But he ignored Nick and cupped Angel's arm, his fingers wrapped all the way around the biceps, whispering in his ear while Nick climbed into the ring. Then Frank hit Angel on the butt and went back to his seat.

Nick danced up and down in his corner, feigning jabs, huffing air out of his nose. "I knew you'd be here," he said.

"I'm your cut man," I said.

"You better believe it," he replied.

As soon as the bell rang, Angel Morales took him apart. It was awful to watch. Angel kidney-punched him in the clenches, opened a cut over Nick's right eye, then headbutted it into a split all along the eyebrow. In the third round he knocked Nick's mouthpiece into the seats, then chopped him against the ropes, driving one punch after another into Nick's exposed face, while sweat showered like diamonds from Nick's hair.

"Stop the fight!" Terry shouted.

"Bullshit! Bullshit!" Nick yelled.

Before the bell for the fourth round I wiped Nick down and tried to dress the cut above his eye, then flapped the towel in his face. His eye was swollen shut and his teeth were pink when I fitted his mouthpiece inside his lips.

"You got to get under his reach," I said.

"I look like a pygmy?" he replied, and tried to grin.

I could hardly watch what Angel did to him in the next round.

In the background, while Nick was being cut to pieces, Frank was talking with his gangster friends, smoking a gold-tipped cigarette, his legs crossed, telling a joke that made them all laugh simultaneously.

Before the round ended I leaned forward over the spit bucket, pretending to pour water onto a fresh towel. Instead, I emptied the water bottle into the bucket, splashing it down the sides, washing the residue of dried bleach into the bottom, where the bar of Lava lay glued to the tin. Then I dropped the towel into the water, soaking it with bleach and soap.

When the bell ended the round I climbed through the ropes with the wood stool, bucket, and towel. I upended the water bottle for Nick to drink, held the bucket for him to spit, then wiped down his chest, forearms, and gloves.

"Bust him in the eyes. Rub your gloves in his eyes. You hear me?" I said.

I doubted if Nick understood what I had done, but when the bell clanged he came hard out of the corner, slipped Angel's first punch, took the second on his shoulder, then unloaded with a right cross that exploded on Angel's nose.

Angel stepped backward, his eyes blinking, as though a flashbulb had popped in his face. Nick jabbed him with his left, then ducked as though going in for a body attack. Angel instinctively tucked in his elbows, covering his stomach, and that's when Nick hooked him in the face with a murderous punch that drenched Angel's eyes with bleach and soap.

Angel stumbled around in the ring, unable to see the punches raining down on him. It didn't take either the crowd or the referee long to figure out what had happened. The crowd began booing, and a cascade of beer cups and half-eaten hot dogs showered into the ring. The referee stopped the fight, and Frank and his friends headed for Nick's corner and me. I was sure I was about to be lynched.

In my mind's eye I saw myself facing them down, shaming Frank Wallace for the degenerate he was, saving Terry Anne and Nick from the mob. But that's not what happened. I kicked the bucket and the soaked towel under the ring apron and ran for my life.

Terry Anne and Nick caught up with me in her car, seven blocks away. Nick was still in his trunks, his face swollen out of shape, his body crawling with stink.

"We screwed the whole bunch of them! It was beautiful! We're gonna be legends! Who needs the Gloves?" he said after I was in the car.

But I saw Terry Anne looking fearfully in the rearview mirror and I knew it was not over.

That night, while kids played softball under the lights at the park and music played through the speakers on the Popsicle truck, I used the pay phone to call the Italian restaurant owned by Mary Jo's family. I put a pencil between my teeth when I spoke.

"Is this Mary Jo Scarlotti's father?" I said.

"I'm her uncle. Who's this?" the voice said.

"A man name of Frank Wallace bothers kids at the park. He's been giving Mary Jo swimming lessons at his apartment. Why don't you people wise up and do something about that?" I said, and hung up, my heart beating.

One year later the Communists would sweep across the thirty-eighth parallel in Korea and Senator Joseph McCarthy and his friends would teach us how to fear one another. Terry Anne would marry a grade-B cowboy actor and open a dude ranch outside of Reno, Nevada. The year after that, Frank Wallace would be found inside a concrete mixer next to the Galveston Freeway.

Maybe my phone call brought about his death. Or maybe not. I didn't care either way. Frank was dead and Mary Jo Scarlotti was valedictorian of our class. The park is still there, little different from the way it was fifty-five years ago. Just the other day I drove past the ball diamond and a group of kids were gathered around an ice cream truck, licking cones and Popsicles, convinced the world was a grand place, full of sun-showers and flowery gardens, inside of which the only purpose of a satyr was to make them laugh.

The Burning

of the Flag

When bombs fell on the ships at Pearl Harbor, we lived on a quiet dead-end street in a city not far from salt water, where palm trees, palmettos, and live oaks grew side by side in meadows that stayed green through the winter months. It was a wonderful street, lined with brick houses, each with a roofed porch, closed off at the end with a cul-du-sac and a dense canebrake, on the other side of which horses grazed in a pasture. On a rainy day, on the far side of the pasture, you could see the lighted tower of a movie theater glowing against the evening sky.

My best friend was Nick Hauser. If it was a time of privation, we did not think of it as such, primarily because no one in our neighborhood had money and most considered themselves fortunate to have survived the Depression years with their families intact. Wake Island and Corregidor fell and we heard terrible stories about the decapitation of American prisoners. But on our block—and that is all we ever called the place we lived, "our block"—the era was marked not so much by a distant war as it was by the presence of radios in people's windows and on their front porches, the visits to the block of the bookmobile and the Popsicle man, and games of street ball and hide-and-seek on summer evenings that smelled of flowers and water sprayed from garden hoses.

One night a week during the summer of 1942 the entire city was blacked out for an air-raid drill. My father sat on the front porch, smoking a cigarette, a white volunteer Civil Defense helmet cocked on his head, sometimes reading the newspaper with a flashlight. Once the drill was over, the theater tower in the distance rippled with neon, and the voices of Fred Allen and Senator Claghorn or Fibber McGee and Molly could be heard all over the neighborhood. I believed no evil would ever enter the quiet world in which we lived.

But if you crossed Westheimer Street, the soft aesthetic blend of the rural South and prewar urban America ended dramatically. On our side of Westheimer was a watermelon stand among giant live oaks, and on the other side of the street a neighborhood of boxlike, utilitarian houses and unkept yards where bitterness and penury were a way of life, and personal failure the fault of black people, Yankees, and foreigners.

The kids on the opposite side of Westheimer gave no quarter in a fight and asked for none in return. Some of them carried switchblades and went nigger-knocking with BB guns and firecrackers. Their cruelty was seldom done in heat but instead visited upon the victim dispassionately, as though the perpetrator were simply passing on an instruction about the way the world worked.

The five Dunlop brothers were legendary in the city's school system. Each of them was a living testimony to the power of the fist or the hobnailed boot over the written word. The youngest and meanest of them was Vernon—two years older than Nick Hauser and me, bullnecked, his lime-green eyes wide-set, his arms always pumped, his body as hard as a man's at age fourteen. He threw an afternoon paper route and set pins side by side with blacks at the bowling alley and as a consequence had more money to spend than we did. But that fact did not make us safe from Vernon Dunlop.

In July and August, Nick Hauser and I picked blackberries and sold them in fat quart jars door-to-door for two bits apiece. Vernon would wait for us on his bicycle behind the watermelon stand, where he knew we would come in the evening, then pelt us with clods of dried clay, never saying a word, sometimes slapping us to the ground, kneeling on one of our chests, frogging our arms and shoulders black and blue. There was neither apparent purpose nor motivation in his attacks. It was just Vernon doing what he did best—making people miserable.

Then one evening he got serious. His lip was puffed and one eye swollen, his forearms streaked with red welts, his T-shirt pulled out of shape at the neck. Obviously, Vernon had just taken a licking from his father or his brothers. While Nick stood by helplessly, Vernon hit me until I cried, twisting his knuckles with each blow, driving the pain deep into the bone. Then I committed one of those cowardly acts that seems to remain inside you forever, like you give up on being you and admit your worthlessness before the world. "I'll give you half my money. The blackberries are for everybody anyway. We should have included you in, Vernon," I said.

"Yeah? That's good of you. Let's see it," he said.

He was still straddled on my chest, but he lifted one knee so I could reach into my trouser pocket. I pressed three quarters into his palm, my eyes locked on his. I felt his weight shift on me, his buttocks and thighs clench me tighter.

He cupped his palm to his mouth, spit a long string of saliva on the coins, and stuffed them inside my shirt, pressing the cloth down on them so they stuck to my skin.

"I just thought of names for you guys," he said. "Nick, you're Snarf. That's a guy who gets his rocks sniffing girls' bicycle seats. Charlie, you're Frump. Don't know what a frump is? A guy who farts in the bathtub and bites the bubbles. Snarf and Frump. Perfect."

He wiped his hand on my shirt as he got off my chest. I

wanted to kill Vernon Dunlop. Instead, I ran home crying, the wet coins still inside my clothes, sure in some perverse fashion that Nick had betrayed me because he had not been Vernon's victim, too.

≈≈≈

That evening I sat by myself at the picnic table in the backyard, throwing a screwdriver end over end into the St. Augustine grass. Our lawn was uncut, the mower propped at an odd angle in the dirt alleyway. I threw the screwdriver hard into the grass, so it embedded almost to the handle in the sod. The kitchen light was on, the window open, and I could hear my parents arguing. The argument was about money or the amount of time my father spent with his friends at the icehouse and beer garden on Alabama Boulevard. I went through the side door into my bedroom, and stuffed my soiled shirt and trousers into the clothes hamper. I bathed and put on my pajamas, and did not tell my parents of what Vernon had done to me. I told my mother I was sick and couldn't eat. Through my screen window I could hear the other kids playing ball in the twilight.

When I woke the next morning, I felt dirty all over, my skin scalded in the places Vernon's saliva had touched it. I was convinced I was a weakling and a moral failure. The song of mockingbirds and the sunlight filtering through the mulberry tree that shaded our driveway seemed created for someone else.

Nick did not come over to play, nor did he come out of

his house when the Popsicle man pedaled his cart down the block that afternoon. At 5:00 p.m. my mother sent me to the icehouse to tell my father it was time for supper. He was talking with three other men about baseball, at a plank table under a striped canopy that flapped in the wind, a bottle of Jax and a small glass and salt shaker in front of him.

He pulled out his pocket watch and looked at it. He had started his vacation that day and had been at the icehouse since noon. "Is it that time already? Well, I bet we still have time for a root beer, don't we?" he said, and told the waiter to bring me a Hires and my father another Jax.

My father was an antithetically mixed, eccentric man who lost his best friend in the trenches on the last day of World War I. He detested war and particularly the demagogues who championed it but had never participated in one themselves. He flew the flag on our front porch, unfurling it from its staff each morning, putting it away in the hall closet at sunset. He taught me how to fold the flag in a tucked square and told me it should never touch the ground or be left in the rain or flown after it had become sun-faded or frayed by the wind. But he attended no veterans' functions, nor would he discuss the current war in front of me or let me look at the photographs of enemy dead that sometimes appeared in *Life* magazine.

My father had wanted to be a journalist, but he had left college without completing his degree and had gone to work for a natural gas pipeline company. After the Crash of '29, any hope of his changing careers was over. He never complained about the work he did, but each day he came home from the job and repeatedly washed his hands, as though he were scrubbing an irremovable stain from fabric.

As we walked home from the icehouse, I asked him if we could go fishing down at Galveston.

"Sure. You want to ask Nick?" he said.

"I don't hang around with Nick anymore," I replied.

"You boys have a fight?"

"No," I replied. Then I felt my mouth flex, waiting for the words to come out that would explain how I let Vernon rub his spit on me and call me Frump, how I gave him half my money just so he would climb off my chest, how I could still feel his scrotum and buttocks pressing against my body.

But I crimped my lips and looked at the cars passing on the street, gas ration stickers glued to their front windows. The light on the trees and lawns and cars seemed to shimmer and break apart.

"You all right, son? You having trouble with the other kids on the block or something?" my father said.

"There's a new kid on the next street from Chicago. He thinks he's better than everybody else. Why doesn't he go back where he came from?" I said.

"Hey, hey," my father said, patting me on the back. "Don't talk about a chum like that. He can't help where he's from. No more of that now, okay?"

"Are we going fishing?"

"We'll see. Your mother has a bunch of things for me to do. Let's take one thing at a time here," my father said.

My parents had a fight that night and my father and I

did not go to Galveston in the morning. In fact, I didn't know where my father went. He was gone for two days, then he came home, unpacked his suitcase, read the newspaper on the front porch, and walked down to the icehouse.

≋

I started to have trouble at school that fall. I had thought of myself as a favorite of the nuns, but on my first six-week report card for the term, the gold stars I had previously received for "attitude" and "conduct" were replaced by green and red ones. To combat wartime scarcity of paper, Sister Agnes examined the Big Chief notebooks of everyone in class. Those who wasted any paper at all were classified as "Germans." Those who wasted egregiously were classified as "Japs." I was designated a Jap.

Later that same day I pushed the boy from Chicago down on the ground and called him a Yankee and a yellowbelly.

In January, the weather turned cold, streaked with rain and smoke from trash fires. The kids in the neighborhood constructed forts from discarded Christmas trees in the pasture at the end of the block, stacking them in front of pits they had dug to make mud balls that they launched with elaborate slingshots they had fashioned from bicycle inner tubes.

But I took no part in the fun. I read the Hardy Boys series I checked out from the bookmobile and listened to

Terry and the Pirates, Captain Midnight, and *Jack Armstrong, the All-American Boy* in the afternoons. Then my mother brought home a box of Wheaties that contained a picture of a Flying Fortress, and a coupon, which, when filled out and returned to the cereal company, would entitle the sender to have his name placed on a scroll inside the fuselage of a United States Air Corps bomber.

My father saw me printing my name on the coupon at the dining-room table. "You sending off for another decoder badge?" he asked.

I explained how my name would be inside a plane that was bombing the Nazis and the Japanese off the map.

"Not a good idea, Charlie. Where'd you get that?" he said.

"Mom brought it home."

"I see," he said. He cracked open a beer in the kitchen and sat down at the table. His package of Lucky Strike cigarettes had a red dot on it with a green circle around the dot.

"Innocent people are dying under those bombs, Charlie. It's not a game," he said.

"I didn't say it was," I replied.

He caught the resentment in my tone and looked at me strangely. "Saw the Christmas-tree forts you boys were building," he said.

"Nick and the others are doing that."

"What's going on, son?"

"They don't like me."

"I don't believe that. Tell you what. Does Nick have a flag for his fort?"

"Flag?"

My father rubbed the top of my head and winked.

Saturday morning he and I walked down to the end of the block and cut through the canebrake into the pasture. It was a fine morning, crisp and sunny, the live oaks by Westheimer puffing with wind. Kids were hunkered down behind their barricades of stacked Christmas trees, lobbing mud balls at one another, a star-spangled kite that a kid had tied to one fort popping against a cloudless blue sky.

The exchange of mud balls stopped when the kids saw my father. Nick came out from behind his fort and looked at us, his faded clothes daubed with dirt, his face hot from play.

"Got room for one more?" my father asked.

"Sure, Mr. Rourke," Nick replied. His eyes didn't meet my father's, and for the first time I realized Nick had been injured by Vernon Dunlop in ways I had not understood.

"Do you fellows want to fly this over your fort?" my father asked, unfurling our flag from its staff.

"That'd be great," Nick said.

"But you've got to take care of it. Don't let it get stained or dirty. Make sure you take it inside when you're done," my father said.

While my father walked back home, Nick and I raised the flag on our ramparts, loaded our slingshots with hard-packed mud balls, and opened fire on the enemy. For just a moment, out of the corner of my eye, I thought I saw

Vernon Dunlop watching us from the grove of oak trees, his muscular thighs forked across the frame of his bicycle.

≈

Nick's father was a decent, religious, blue-collar man who built a clubhouse for us in one of the live oak trees on West-heimer and sometimes walked us to the Alabama Theater on Friday nights. The family did not own a car and Nick's father rode the city bus to his job as a supervisor at a laun-dry on the north side of downtown. He had been a Golden Gloves boxer as a teenager in Mobile, and he owned a set of sixteen-ounce boxing gloves that he used in teaching Nick and the other kids to box. But he was a strict discipli-narian and admonished his children to never bring home a mark on their bodies that God didn't put there. When he took out his razor strop, Nick's scalp would literally recede on his head, as though it had been exposed to a naked flame.

At the end of the first afternoon we had flown the flag at the fort, Nick rolled the flag on its staff and handed it to me.

"My dad wants you to keep it at your house," I said.

"Is your dad mad at me?" Nick asked. His dark hair was buzz-cut, his skin still brown from summer, his face round, his cheeks pooled with color. There were dirt rings on his neck, and I could smell the heat and dampness in his clothes from playing all day.

"Why would my dad be mad at you?"

"I didn't help you when Vernon rubbed his spit on you."

I felt my eyes film at the image he had used. "I didn't tell my dad anything," I said.

"When I get bigger, I'm gonna break Vernon's nose. He's not so tough with big guys," he said.

But Vernon was tough with big guys. We found that out the next week when Nick and I started our first afternoon paper route together. The paper corner where the bundles were dropped for the carriers was across Westheimer. Not only was it a block from Vernon's house, it was the same corner where Vernon and his brothers rolled the papers for their route. I couldn't believe our bad luck. We sat on the pavement, our legs splayed, rolling our papers into cylinders, whipping mouth-wet string around them to cinch them tight, while Vernon did the same three feet from us.

A jalopy packed with north side kids, the top cut away with an acetylene torch, ran the stop sign, all of them shooting the bone at everyone on the corner. They parked by the drugstore and went inside, lighting cigarettes, running combs through their ducktails, squeezing their scrotums. Vernon got on his bicycle, one with no tire guards and a wood rack for his canvas saddlebags, and rode down to the drugstore. He calmly parked his bike on its kickstand, flicked opened his switchblade, and sliced off the valve stems on all four of the jalopy's tires.

Ten minutes later, when the jalopy's occupants came out of the drugstore, Vernon was back on the corner, rolling his papers. They stared at their tires, unable to believe what they were seeing. So they would make no mistake about who had done the damage to them, Vernon stood up, shot them the bone with both hands, followed by the Italian salute and the eat-shit horns of the cuckold sign. Then he bent over and mooned them and shot them the bone again, this time between his legs.

He took a tire iron from his saddlebags and clanked it on a fireplug until the northsiders got back in their jalopy and drove it on the rims out of the neighborhood.

For a moment I almost felt Vernon was our ally. He disabused us of that notion by hanging Nick's bicycle on a telephone spike fifteen feet above the street.

≈≈≈

That spring, Nick and I collected old newspapers, coat hangers, tinfoil, and discarded rubber tires for the war effort, and hauled them down to the collection center at the fire station. We used baling wire to attach the staff of our flag to the wooden slats on the side of Nick's wagon and worked our way up and down alleys throughout the neighborhood, the wagon creaking under the load of junk stacked inside it, confident that in some fashion we were fighting the forces of evil that had bombed Pearl Harbor, Warsaw, and Coventry.

At the outset of the war, families in our neighborhood had hung small service flags in their windows—blue stars on a white field, inside a rectangle of blue and red—indicating the number of men and women from that home who had gone to war. Now, in the spring of '43, some of the blue stars had been replaced by gold ones.

The Sweeney boy from across the street parachuted into Europe and eventually would be one of the soldiers who captured Hitler's fortified chalet at Berchtesgaden. My cousin Weldon gave up his ROTC deferment at Texas A&M and came home with the Silver Star, three Purple Hearts, and one lung. Nick and I began to collect meat drippings from people's kitchens and take them to the local butcher, who supposedly shipped them in large barrels to a munitions factory where they were made into nitroglycerine. Everyone in the neighborhood knew us by the flag on our wagon. My father's friends at the icehouse bought us cold drinks. Nick and I glowed with pride.

"Y'all think your shit don't stink?" Vernon said to us one day on the paper corner.

Nick and I buried our faces in our work, rolling the top newspapers on the stack, whipping string around them, pitching them heavily into the saddlebags on our bikes. Vernon grabbed my wrist, stopping me in mid-roll. "Which one are you—Frump or Snarf?" he asked.

"I'm Frump," I said.

"Then answer my question, Frump."

"My shit stinks, Vernon," I said.

"You a wiseass?" Vernon said.

"Why don't you leave him alone?" Nick said.

"What'd you say?" Vernon asked.

The only sounds on the corner were the wind in the trees and a milk truck rattling down the street.

"Your brothers went to the pen. That's why they're not in the army. Charlie's cousin won the Silver Star. I heard your sister dosed the yardman," Nick said.

I could hear the words *no, no, no* like a drumbeat in my head.

"Tell me, Snarf, did you know Hauser is a Kraut name?" Vernon said.

"My dad says it's a lot better than being white trash," Nick said.

Vernon lit a cigarette and puffed on it thoughtfully, then flicked the hot match into Nick's eye.

After we threw the route, I put my bike away in the garage and walked unexpectedly through the back door of the house, into the kitchen, where my mother and father were fighting. They both looked at me blankly, like people in whose faces a flashbulb had just popped.

"Why y'all got to fight all the time?" I said.

"You mustn't talk like that. We were just having a discussion," my mother said. There was baking flour on her hands and arms and a smudge of it on her cheek.

I went back outside and threw rocks into the canebrake at the end of the street, and did not go home for supper. At sunset, Nick and I sat in the tree house we had built on the edge of Westheimer and watched the electric lights come on in the oak grove where the watermelon stand was. Vernon's father, with two of his older sons, crossed the street and sat down at one of the tables, a cigar between his fingers, his bald head faintly iridescent, like an alabaster bowling ball. The smoke from his cigar drifted onto another table, causing a family to move. His sons cut in line by pretending they were with a friend, and brought chunks of melon, as red as freshly sliced meat, back to the table. The three of them began eating, spitting their seeds into the grass.

"I hope the Dunlops go to hell," I said.

"Sister Agnes says that's a mortal sin," Nick replied. Then he grinned. The burn on his face looked like a tiny yellow bug under his eye. "Maybe they'll just go to purgatory and never get out."

"You stood up for me and I didn't try to help you," I said.

"It wouldn't have done any good. Vernon can whip both of us."

"You were brave. You're a lot braver than me," I said.

"Who cares about Vernon Dunlop? I got a dime. Let's get a cold drink at the filling station," Nick said.

Through the slats of the tree house I could see the Dunlops slurping down their watermelon. "I don't feel too good. I don't feel good about anything," I said.

"Don't be like that, Charlie. We'll always be pals," Nick said.

I climbed down the tree trunk and dropped into the tannic smell of leaves that had turned black with the spring rains and that broke with a wet, snapping sound under my feet. Out in the darkness I heard horses blowing and I could see lightning flicker like veins of quicksilver in a bank of storm heads over the Gulf of Mexico. But the nocturnal softness of the season had no influence on my heart and a few minutes later I knew that was the way things would go from there on out. When I got home, my father was gone. That night I slept with my pillow crimped down tightly on my head.

Early Saturday morning, Nick knocked on my screen window. He was barefoot and wore short pants, and his face looked unwashed and full of sleep.

"What is it?" I whispered.

"The flag. It's gone," he replied.

"Gone?"

"I left it on the wagon. I forgot to take it in last night," he said.

We stared through the screen into each other's faces. "Vernon?" I said.

"Who else?" Nick replied.

I spent the entire day locked inside my own head, my throat constricted with fear at the prospect of confronting Vernon Dunlop. My father had not returned home and I went to the icehouse to see if I could find him. His friends were kindly toward me, and when they sat me down and bought me a cold drink and a hot dog, I knew they possessed knowledge about my life that I didn't.

I tried to convince myself that someone other than Vernon had stolen the flag. Maybe it had been one of the colored yardmen who worked in the neighborhood, or the Cantonese kids whose parents ran a small grocery up on Westheimer. Maybe I had been unfair to Vernon. Why blame him for every misdeed in the neighborhood?

At dusk I rode my bike down his street, my heart in my throat, as though at any moment he would burst from the quiet confines of his frame house, one that was painted the same shade of yellow as the buildings in the Southern Pacific freight yards. A dead pecan tree stood in the front yard, the rotted gray ropes of a swing with no seat lifting in the breeze. Inside the house someone was listening to *Gangbusters,* police sirens and staccato bursts of machine-gun fire erupting behind the announcer's voice. But no American flag flew from the Dunlops' house.

I made a turn at the end of block and headed back home on a street parallel to Vernon's, temporarily triumphant over my fears. Then, through a space between two dilapidated garages, I saw our flag and staff nailed at a forty-five-degree angle to a post on the Dunlops' back porch.

I pedaled straight ahead, my eyes fixed on the intersection, my face stinging as though it had been slapped. I wanted to find Nick or go look for my father again, or to get hit by a car or do anything that would remove me from what I knew I had to do next. The sun was a molten ball now, buried inside a strip of purple cloud, the sky freckled with birds. I turned my bike around and rode back down the alleyway to the Dunlops' house, through lines of garbage cans, my heart hammering in my ears.

Then a peculiar event happened inside me. Like the stories I had heard on the radio of a soldier going over a parapet into Japanese machine-gun fire or an aviator with no parachute leaping from his burning plane, I surrendered myself to my fate and crossed the Dunlops' yard to their back porch. With my hands shaking, I pried the flagstaff from the wood post, the nail wrenching free as loudly as a rusted hinge, and walked quickly between the Dunlops' garage and the neighbor's to my bicycle, rolling the flag on its staff, confident I had rescued the flag intact.

I stuffed it in one of my saddlebags and kicked my bike stand back into place. Just as I did, I saw Mr. Dunlop shove Vernon from the back door of the house into the yard. Mr. Dunlop wore a strap undershirt and blue serge pants, and he had a dog chain doubled around his fist. He whipped his son with it four times across the back, then threw him to the ground.

"You stole money out of a nigger's house? Don't lie or I'll take the hide off you for real," Mr. Dunlop said.

"Yes, Daddy," Vernon replied, weeping, his face powdered with dust.

I thought his father was going to hit Vernon again, but he didn't. "Folks is gonna say we're so hard up you got to steal from niggers. What we gonna do with you, son?" he said.

Then he sat down on the step and stroked Vernon's head as though he were petting a dog. "What are you looking at?" he said to me.

I crossed Westheimer and pushed my bike through the

oak grove by the watermelon stand and followed the path through the canebrake to Nick's house. I knocked on the door, then unfurled the flag as I waited. My heart dropped when I saw the streaks of grease and dirt and pinlike separations across one side of the cloth, printed there, I suspected, by the chain or spokes of Vernon's bicycle. But he had hung it from his porch anyway, like a scalp rather than the symbol of his country.

Nick opened the screen door and stepped outside. "Wow! You got it back. You slam ole Vernon upside the head with a brick or something?" he said.

"It's ruined," I replied.

Nick placed his hand on the bottom side of the cloth. The pinkness of his palm showed through the separations in the thread. "What are we gonna do?" he said.

≋

My father had taught me not only how to care for the flag but also how to dispose of it if it was soiled or damaged. That night, Nick and I conducted a private ceremony under our tree house. We built a fire of grass and decayed oak limbs, and spread our stained flag on top of the flames. We stood at attention like toy soldiers and saluted the thick curds of smoke and black threads of cloth that rose out of the heat, some of them sparking like fireflies among the oaks where people were still eating watermelon. Someone called the fire department, and the owner of the watermelon stand told us he would have our tree house torn down. Almost simultaneously Mr. Dunlop and his sons showed up, enraged that I had stolen and destroyed *their* flag.

It was a year of Allied naval victories in the Pacific, rationing about which no one complained, and Tommy Dorsey and Glenn Miller on the jukebox. It was the year in which a group of good-natured firemen and the Dunlop family and the patrons of a watermelon stand stood in a circle around two small boys, like creatures whose exteriors were made of tallow, warping in the firelight, exposing for good or bad the child that lives in us all.

It was 1943, the year my father died in a duck-hunting accident down at Anahuac and the year Nick Hauser and I beat the world and never told anybody about it.

Why Bugsy Siegel Was
a Friend of Mine

In 1947, Nick Hauser and I had only two loves in this world—baseball and Cheerio yo-yo contests. That's how we met Benny, one spring night after a double-header out at Buffalo Stadium on the Galveston Freeway. His brand-new Ford convertible, a gleaming maroon job with a starch-white top, whitewall tires, and blue-dot taillights, was stuck in a sodden field behind the bleachers. Benny was trying to lift the bumper while his girlfriend floored the accelerator, spinning the tires and blowing streams of muddy water and torn grass back in his face.

He wore a checkered sport coat, lavender shirt, hand-painted necktie, and two-tone shoes, all of it now whip-sawed with mud. But it was his eyes, not his clothes, that you remembered. They were a radiant blue and literally sparkled.

"You punks want to earn two bucks each?" he said.

"Who you calling a punk?" Nick said.

Before Benny could answer, his girlfriend shifted into reverse, caught traction, and backed over his foot.

He hopped up and down, holding one shin, trying to bite down on his pain, his eyes lifted heavenward, his lips moving silently.

"Get in the fucking car before it sinks in this slop again!" his girlfriend yelled.

He limped to the passenger side. A moment later they fishtailed across the grass past us. Her hair was long, blowing out the window, the pinkish-red of a flamingo. She thumbed a hot cigarette into the darkness.

"Boy, did you check out that babe's bongos? Wow!" Nick said.

But our evening encounter with Benny and his girl-friend was not over. We were on the shoulder of the free-way, trying to hitch a ride downtown, flicking our Cheerios under a streetlamp, doing a whole range of upper-level yo-yo tricks—round-the-world, shoot-the-moon, rock-the-cradle, and the atomic bomb—when the maroon convert-ible roared past us, blowing dust and newspaper in our faces.

Suddenly the convertible cut across two lanes of traffic,

made a U-turn, then a second U-turn, horns blowing all over the freeway, and braked to a stop abreast of us.

"You know who I am?" Benny said.

"No," I replied.

"My name is Benjamin Siegel."

"You're a gangster," Nick said.

"He's got you, Benny," the woman behind the wheel said.

"How you know that?" Benny said.

"We heard your name on *Gangbusters.* Nick and me listen every Saturday night," I said.

"Can you do the Chinese star?" he asked.

"We do Chinese stars in our sleep," Nick said.

"Get in," Benny said, pulling back the leather seat.

"We got to get home," I said.

"We'll take you there. Get in," he said.

We drove out South Main, past Rice University and parklike vistas dense with live oak trees, some of them hung with Spanish moss. In the south, heat lightning flickered over the Gulf of Mexico. Benny bought us fried chicken and ice cream at Bill Williams Drive-In, and while we ate, his girlfriend smoked cigarettes behind the wheel and listened to the radio, her thoughts known only to herself, her face so soft and lovely in the dash light I felt something drop inside me when I stole a look at it.

Benny popped open the glove box and removed a top-of-the-line chartreuse Cheerio yo-yo. Behind the yo-yo I could see the steel surfaces of a semiautomatic pistol. "Now show me the Chinese star," he said.

He stood with us in the middle of the drive-in parking lot, watching Nick and me demonstrate the intricate patterns of the most difficult of all the Cheerio competition tricks. Then he tried it himself. His yo-yo tilted sideways, its inner surfaces brushing against the string, then twisted on itself and went dead.

"The key is candle wax," I said.

"Candle wax?" he said.

"Yeah, you wrap the string around a candle and saw it back and forth. That gives you the spin and the time you need to make the pattern for the star," I said.

"I never thought of that," he said.

"It's a breeze," Nick said.

"Benny, give it a rest," his girlfriend said from inside the car.

Fifteen minutes later, we dropped off Nick at his house on the dead-end street where I used to be his neighbor. It was a wonderful street, one of trees and flowers and old brick homes, and a horse pasture dotted with live oaks beyond the canebrake that enclosed the cul-du-sac. But when my father died, my mother and I were evicted, and we moved across Westheimer and took up residence in a neighborhood where every sunrise broke on the horizon like a testimony to personal failure.

Benny's girlfriend pulled to a stop in front of my house. Benny looked at the broken porch and the orange rust on the screens. "This is where you live?" he asked.

"Yeah," I said, my eyes leaving his.

He nodded. "You need to study hard, make something of yourself. Go out to California, maybe. It's the place to be," he said.

≋

Our next-door neighbors were the Dunlops. They had skin like pig hide and heads with the knobbed ridges of coconuts. The oldest of the five boys was executed in Huntsville Pen; one did time on Sugarland Farm.

The patriarch of the family was a security guard at the Southern Pacific train yards. He covered all the exterior surfaces of his house, garage, and toolshed with the yellow paint he stole from his employer. The Dunlops even painted their car with it. Then through a fluke no one could have anticipated, they became rich.

One of the girls had married a morphine addict who came from an oil family in River Oaks. The girl and her husband drove their Austin Healey head-on into a bus outside San Antonio, and the Dunlops inherited two hundred thousand dollars and a huge chunk of rental property in their own neighborhood. It was like giving a tribe of Pygmies a nuclear weapon.

I thought the Dunlops would move out of their dilapidated two-story frame house, with its piles of dog shit all over the backyard, but instead they bought a used Cadillac from a mortuary, covered their front porch with glitter-encrusted chalk animals and icons from an amusement park, and each morning continued to piss out the attic window on my mother's car, which looked like it had contracted scabies.

As newly empowered landlords, the Dunlops cut no one any slack, did no repairs on their properties, and evicted a Mexican family that had lived in the neighborhood since the mid-Depression. Mr. Dunlop also seized upon an opportunity to repay the parochial school Nick and I attended for expelling two of his sons.

Maybe it was due to the emotional deprivation and the severity of the strictures imposed upon them, or the black habits they wore in ninety-degree humidity, but a significant number of the nuns at school were inept and cruel. Sister Felicie, however, was not one of these. She was tall, and wore steel-rimmed glasses and small black shoes that didn't seem adequate to support her height. When I spent almost a year in bed with rheumatic fever, she came every other day to the house with my lessons, walking a mile, sometimes in the hottest of weather, her habit powdered with ash from a burned field she had to cross.

But things went south for Sister Felicie. We heard that her father, a senior army officer, was killed at Okinawa. Others said the soldier was not her father but the fiancé she had given up when she entered the convent. Regardless, at the close of the war a great sadness seemed to descend upon her.

In the spring of '47, she would take her science class on a walk through the neighborhood, identifying trees, plants, and flowers along the way. Then, just before 3:00 p.m., we

would end up at Costen's Drugstore, and she would let
everyone take a rest break on the benches under the
awning. It was a grand way to end the school day, because
on some afternoons the Cheerio yo-yo man would arrive at
exactly 3:05 and hold competitions on the corner.

But one day, just after the dismissal bell had rung across
the street, I saw Sister Felicie walk into the alleyway between the drugstore and Cobb's Liquors and give money to
a black man who had an empty eye socket. A few minutes
later I saw her upend a small bottle of fortified wine, what
hobos used to call short-dogs, then drop it surreptitiously
into a trash can.

She turned and realized I had been watching her. She
walked toward me, between the old brick walls of the buildings, her small shoes clicking on pieces of gravel and bottle
caps and broken glass, her face stippled with color inside
her wimple. "Why aren't you waxing your string for the
Cheerio contest?" she said.

"It hasn't started yet, Sister," I replied, avoiding her
look, trying to smile.

"Better run on now," she said.

"Are you all right, Sister?" I said, then wanted to bite off
my tongue.

"Of course I'm all right. Why do you ask?"

"No reason. None. I just don't think too good sometimes, Sister. You know me. I was just—"

But she wasn't listening now. She walked past me toward the red light at the corner, her habit and beads swishing against my arm. She smelled like camphor and booze

and the lichen in the alley she had bruised under her small shoes.

Two days later, the same ritual repeated itself. Except this time Sister Felicie didn't empty just one short-dog and head for the convent. I saw her send the black man back to Cobb's for two more bottles, then she sat down on a rusted metal chair at the back of the alley, a book spread on her knees, as though she were reading, the bottles on the ground barely hidden by the hem of her habit.

That's when Mr. Dunlop and his son Vernon showed up. Vernon was seventeen and by law could not be made to attend school. That fact was a gift from God to the educational system of southwest Houston. Vernon had half-moon scars on his knuckles, biceps the size of small muskmelons, and deep-set simian eyes that focused on other kids with the moral sympathies of an electric drill.

Mr. Dunlop was thoroughly enjoying himself. First, he announced to everyone within earshot he was the owner of the entire corner, including the drugstore. He told the Cheerio yo-yo man to beat it and not come back, then told the kids to either buy something inside the store or get off the benches they were loitering on.

His face lit like a jack-o'-lantern's when he saw Sister Felicie emerge from the alley. She was trying to stand straight, and not doing a very good job of it, one hand touching the brick wall of the drugstore, a drop of sweat running from the top edge of her wimple down the side of her nose.

"Looks like you got a little bit of the grog in you, Sister," Mr. Dunlop said.

"What were you saying to the children?" she asked.

"Oh, her ladyship wants to know that, does she? Why don't we have a conference with the pastor and hash it out?" Mr. Dunlop said.

"Do as you wish," Sister replied, then walked to the red light with the cautious steps of someone aboard a pitching ship.

Mr. Dunlop dropped a Buffalo nickel into a pay phone, an unlit cigarette in the corner of his mouth. His head was shaved bald, his brow knurled, one eye recessed and glistening with pleasure when someone picked up on the other end. "Father?" Mr. Dunlop said.

His son Vernon squeezed his scrotum and shot us the bone.

≈≈≈

The Cheerio yo-yo man did not come back to the corner and Sister Felicie disappeared from school for a week. Then one Monday morning she was back in class, looking joyless and glazed, as though she had just walked out of an ice storm.

That afternoon, Benny and his girlfriend pulled into my driveway while I was picking up the trash Vernon and his brothers had thrown out of their attic window into the yard. "I can't get the atomic bomb right. Get in the car. We'll pick up your friend on the way out," he said.

"Way where?" I said.

"The Shamrock. You want to go swimming and have some eats, don't you?" he said.

"I'll leave my mom a note," I said.

"Tell her to come out and join us."

That definitely will not flush, I thought, but did not say it.

Benny had said he couldn't pull off the yo-yo trick called the atomic bomb. The truth was he couldn't even master walk-the-dog. In fact, I couldn't figure why a man with his wealth and criminal reputation would involve himself so intensely with children's games. After Nick and I went swimming, we sat on the balcony of Benny's suite, high above the clover-shaped pool of the Shamrock Hotel, and tried to show him the configurations of the atomic bomb. It was a disaster. He would spread the string between his fingers, then drop the yo-yo through the wrong spaces, knotting the string, rendering it useless. He danced up and down on the balls of his feet in frustration.

"There's something wrong with this yo-yo. I'm gonna go back to the guy who sold it to me and stuff it down his throat," he said.

"He's full of shit, kids," his girlfriend said through the open bathroom door.

"Don't listen to that. You're looking at the guy who almost blew up Mussolini," he said to us. Then he yelled through the French doors into the suite, "Tell me I'm full of shit one more time."

"You're full of shit," she yelled back.

"That's what you got to put up with," he said to us. "Now, teach me the atomic bomb."

Blue-black clouds were piled from the horizon all the

way to the top of the sky, blooming with trees of lightning that made no sound. Across the street, we could see oil rigs pumping in an emerald-green pasture and a half-dozen horses starting to spook at the weather. Benny's girlfriend came out of the bathroom, dressed in new jeans and a black and maroon cowboy shirt with a silver stallion on the pocket. She drank from a vodka collins, and her mouth looked cold and hard and beautiful when she lowered the glass.

"Anybody hungry?" she said.

I felt myself swallow. Then, for reasons I didn't understand, I told her and Benny what Mr. Dunlop had done to Sister Felicie. Benny listened attentively, his handsome face clouding, his fingers splaying his knotted yo-yo string in different directions. "Say all that again? This guy Dunlop ran off the Cheerio man?" he said.

It was almost Easter, and at school that meant the Stations of the Cross and a daily catechism reminder about the nature of disloyalty and human failure. When he needed them most, Christ's men bagged it down the road and let him take the weight on his own. I came to appreciate the meaning of betrayal a little better that spring.

I thought my account of Mr. Dunlop's abuse of Sister Felicie and the Cheerio man had made Benny our ally. He'd said he would come by my house the next night and straighten out Mr. Dunlop and anyone else who was pushing around kids and nuns and yo-yo instructors. He said these kinds of guys were Nazis and should be boiled into lard and poured into soap molds. He said, "Don't worry, kid. I owe you guys. You taught me the atomic bomb and the Chinese star."

The next day, after school, when I was raking leaves in the yard, Vernon used his slingshot to shoot me in the back with a marble. I felt the pain go into the bone like a cold chisel.

"Got a crick?" he said.

"Yeah," I said mindlessly, squeezing my shoulders back, my eyes shut.

"How about some hair of the dog that bit you?" he said, fishing another marble out of his shirt pocket.

"You screwed with Benny Siegel, Vernon. He's going to stuff you in a toilet bowl," I said.

"Yeah? Who is Benny Sea Gull?"

"Ask your old man. Oh, I forgot. He can't read, either."

Vernon's fist came out of the sky and knocked me to the ground. I felt my breath go out of my chest as though it were being sucked into a giant vacuum cleaner. Through the kitchen window, I could see my mother washing dishes, her face bent down toward the sink. Vernon unbuckled my belt, worked the top button loose on my jeans, and pulled them off my legs, dragging me through the dust. The clouds, trees, garage, alleyway, even the dog dumps spun in circles around me. Vernon pulled one of my pants legs inside out and used it to blow his nose.

Benny and his girlfriend did not show up at my house

that night. I called the Shamrock Hotel and asked for his room.

"There's no one registered here by that name," the clerk said.

"Has he checked out?"

There was a pause. "We have no record of a guest with that name. I'm sorry. Thank you for calling the Shamrock," the clerk said, and hung up.

≈≈

The next day at recess I saw Sister Felicie sitting on a stone bench under a live oak in a garden behind the church. Her black habit was spangled with sunlight, and her beads lay across her open palm as though the wind had robbed her of her concentration. Her face looked like ceramic, polished, faintly pink, not quite real. She smelled of soap or perhaps shampoo in her close-cropped hair, which was covered with a skullcap and veil that must have been unbearable in the summer months.

"You're supposed to be on the playground, Charlie," she said.

"I told Benny Siegel what Mr. Dunlop did to you. He promised to help. But he didn't show up last night," I said.

"What are you talking about?"

"Benny is a gangster. Nick and I have been teaching him yo-yo tricks. He built a casino in Nevada."

"I'm convinced you'll be a great writer one day," she said, and for the first time in weeks she smiled. "You're a good boy, Charlie. I may not see you again, at least for a while. But you'll be in my prayers."

"Not see you?"

"Run along now. Don't hang out with too many gangsters."

She patted me on top of the head, then touched my cheek.

≋

Benny had shown Nick and me color photographs of the resort hotel and gambling casino he had built in the desert. He also showed us a picture of him and his girlfriend building a snowman in front of a log cabin in West Montana. In the photograph she was smiling and looked much younger, somehow innocent among evergreens that rang with winter light. She wore a fluffy pink sweater and knee-high boots stitched with Christmas designs.

I kept wanting to believe Benny would call or come by, but he didn't. I dreamed about a building in a desert, its exterior scrolled with neon, a grassy pond on one side of it where flamingos stood in the water, arching their necks, pecking at the insects in their feathers.

I put away my Cheerio yo-yo and no longer listened to ball games at Buffalo Stadium. I refused to eat, without understanding why, threw my lunch in a garbage can on the way to school, and fantasized about hurting Vernon Dunlop.

"We'll set fire to his house," Nick said.

"Serious?" I said, looking up from the box of shoes we were shining in his garage.

"It's a thought," he replied.

"What if somebody gets killed?"

"That's the breaks when you're white trash," Nick said. He grinned, his face full of play. He had a burr haircut and the overhead light reflected on his scalp. Nick was a good boxer, swallowed his blood in a fight, and never let anyone know when he was hurt. Secretly I always wished I was as tough as he was.

He and I had a shoeshine route. We collected shoes from all over the neighborhood and shined them for ten cents a pair, using only one color polish—brown; home delivery was free.

Nick peeled a Milky Way and bit into it. He chewed thoughtfully, then offered the candy bar to me. I shook my head.

"You got to eat," he said.

"Who says?" I replied.

"You make me sad, Charlie," he said.

≋

My father had been an old-time pipeline man whose best friend was killed by his side on the last day of World War I. He read classical literature, refused to mow the lawn under any circumstances, spent more days than he should in the beer joint, attended church irregularly, and contended there were only two facts you had to remember about the nature of God—that He had a sense of humor and, as a gentleman, He never broke His word.

The last part always stuck with me.

Benny had proved himself a liar and a bum. My sense of having been used by him seemed to grow daily. My mother could not make me eat, even when my hunger was eating its way through my insides like a starving organism that had to consume its host in order to survive. I had bed spins when I woke in the morning and vertigo when I rode my bike to school, wobbling between automobiles while the sky, trees, and buildings around me dissolved into a vortex of atomic particles.

My mother tried to tempt me from my abstinence with a cake she baked and the following day with a codfish din-ner she brought from the cafeteria, wrapped in foil, butter oozing from an Irish potato that was still hot from the oven.

I rushed from the house and pedaled my bike to Nick's. We sat inside the canebrake at the end of our old street, while the day cooled and the evening star twinkled in the west. There was a bitter taste in my mouth, like the taste of zinc pennies.

"You miss your dad?" Nick asked.

"I don't think about it much anymore. It was an acci-dent. Why go around feeling bad about an accident?" I replied, turning my face from his, looking at the turquoise rim along the bottom of the sky.

"My old man always says your dad was stand-up."

"Benny Siegel treated us like jerks, Nick," I said.

"Who cares about Benny Siegel?"

I didn't have an answer for him, nor could I explain why I felt the way I did.

I rode my bike home in the dusk, then found a heavy rock in the alley and threw it against the side of the Dunlops' house. It struck the wood so hard the glass in the windows rattled. Vernon came out on the back porch, eating a piece of fried chicken, his body silhouetted in the kitchen light. He wore a strap undershirt and his belt was unbuckled, hanging loosely over his fly.

"You're lucky, dick-wipe. I got a date tonight. But wait till tomorrow," he said. He shook his chicken bone at me.

≋

I couldn't sleep that night. I had terrible dreams about facing Vernon in the morning. How could I have been so foolish as to actually assault his house? I wished I had taken the pounding right then, when I was in hot blood and not trembling with fear. I woke at 2:00 a.m. and threw up in the toilet, then went into the dry heaves. I lay in bed, my head under the pillow. I prayed an asteroid would crash into our neighborhood so I wouldn't have to see the sunrise.

At around five o'clock I fell asleep. Later I heard wind rattle the roof, then a loud knocking sound like a door slamming repeatedly on a doorjamb. When I looked out my screen window, I could see fog on the street and a maroon convertible with whitewall tires parked in front of the Dunlops' house. An olive-skinned man with patent-leather hair, parted down the middle, wearing a clip-on bow tie and crinkling white shirt, sat in the passenger seat. I rubbed my eyes. It was the Cheerio man Mr. Dunlop had run off from the parking lot in front of Costen's Drugstore. Then I heard Benny's voice on the Dunlops' porch.

"See, you can't treat people like that. This is the United States, not Mussoliniville. So we need to walk out here and apologize to this guy and invite him back to the corner by the school. You're good with that, aren't you?"

There was a gap in the monologue. Then Benny's voice resumed. "You're not? You're gonna deny kids the right to enter Cheerio yo-yo contests? You think all those soldiers died in the war for nothing? That's what you're saying? You some kind of Nazi pushing around little people? Look at me when I'm talking, here."

Then Benny and Mr. Dunlop walked out to the convertible and talked to the Cheerio man. A moment later, Benny got behind the wheel and the convertible disappeared in the fog.

I fell sound asleep in the deep blue coolness of the room, with a sense of confidence in the world I had not felt since the day the war ended and Kate Smith's voice sang "God Bless America" from every radio in the neighborhood.

When I woke, it was hot and bright outside, the wind touched with dust and the stench of melted tar. I told my mother of Benny Siegel's visit to the Dunlops.

"You must have had a dream, Charlie. I was up early. I would have heard," she said.

"No, it was Benny. His girlfriend wasn't with him, but the Cheerio man was."

She smiled wanly, her eyes full of pity. "You've starved yourself and you break my heart. Nobody was out there, Charlie. *Nobody,*" she said.

I went out to the curb. No one ever parked in front of the Dunlops' house, and because the sewer drain was clogged, a patina of mud always dried along the edge of the gutter after each rain. I walked out in the street so I wouldn't be on the Dunlops' property, my eyes searching along the seam between the asphalt and the gutter. But I could see no tire imprint in the gray film left over from the last rain. I knelt down and touched the dust with my fingers.

Vernon opened his front door and held it back on the spring. He was bare-chested, a pair of sweatpants tied below his navel. "Losing your marbles, Frump?" he asked.

By noon, my skin was crawling with anxiety and fear. Worse, I felt an abiding shame in the fact that once again I had been betrayed by my own vanity and foolish trust in others. I didn't care anymore whether Vernon beat me up or not. In fact, I wanted to see myself injured. Through the kitchen window I could see him pounding dust out of a rug on the wash line with a broken tennis racquet. I walked down the back steps and crossed into his yard. "Vernon?" I said.

"Your butt-kicking appointment is after lunch. I'm busy right now. In the meantime, entertain yourself by giving a blow job to a doorknob," he replied.

"This won't take long," I said.

He turned around, exasperated. I hit him, hard, on the corner of the mouth, with a right cross that Nick Hauser would have been proud of. It broke Vernon's lip against his teeth, whipping his face sideways, causing him to drop the racquet. He stared at me in disbelief, a string of spittle and blood on his cheek. Before he could raise his hands, I hit him again, this time square on the nose. I felt it flatten and blood fly under my knuckles, then I caught him in the eye and throat. I took one in the side of the head and felt another slide off my shoulder, but I was under his reach now and I got him again in the mouth, this time hurting him more than he was willing to live with.

He stepped back from me, blood draining from his split lip, his teeth red, his face twitching with shock. Out of the corner of my eye, I saw his father appear on the back porch.

"Get in here, boy, before I whup your ass worse than it already is," Mr. Dunlop said.

≈≈≈

That afternoon, Nick Hauser and I went to a baseball game at Buffalo Stadium. When I came home, my mother told me I had received a long-distance telephone call. This was in an era when people only called long distance to inform family members that a loved one had died. I called the operator and was soon connected to Sister Felicie. She told me she was back at Our Lady of the Lake, the college in San Antonio where she had trained to become a teacher.

"I appreciate what your friend has tried to do, but would you tell him everything is fine now, that he doesn't need to act on my behalf anymore?" she said.

"Which friend?" I asked.

"Mr. Siegel. He's called the archdiocese twice." I heard her laugh, then clear her throat. "Can you do that for me, Charlie?"

≋

But I never saw Benny or his girlfriend again. In late June, I read in the newspaper that Benny had been at her cottage in Beverly Hills, reading the *Los Angeles Times,* when someone outside propped an M-1 carbine across the fork of a tree and fired directly into Benny's face, blowing one eye fifteen feet from his head.

Years later, I would read a news story about his girlfriend, whose nickname was the Flamingo, and how she died by suicide in a snowbank in Austria. I sometimes wondered if in those last moments of her life she tried to return to that wintertime photograph of her and Benny building a snowman in West Montana.

Vernon Dunlop never bothered me again. In fact, I came to have a sad kind of respect for the type of life that had been imposed upon him. Vernon was killed at the Battle of Inchon during the Korean War. Nick Hauser and I became schoolteachers. The era in which we grew up was a poem and Bugsy Siegel was a friend of mine.

Jesus
Out to Sea

 I grew up in the Big Sleazy, uptown, off Magazine, amongst live oak trees and gangsters and musicians and bougainvillea the Christian Brothers said was put there to remind us of Christ's blood in the Garden of Gethsemane.

My best friends were Tony and Miles Cardo. Their mother made her living shampooing the hair of corpses in a funeral parlor on Tchoupitoulas. I was with them the afternoon they found a box of human arms someone at the Tulane medical school left by the campus incinerator. Tony stuffed the arms in a big bag of crushed ice, and the next day, at five o'clock, when all the employees from the cigar factory were loading onto the St. Claude streetcar, him and Miles hung the arms from hand straps and the backs of seats all over the car. People started screaming their heads off and clawing their way out the doors. A big fat black guy climbed out the window and crashed on top of a sno-ball cart. Tony and Miles, those guys were a riot.

Tony was known as the Johnny Wadd of the Mafia because he had a flopper on him that looked like a fifteen-inch chunk of radiator hose. All three of us joined the Crotch and went to Vietnam, but Tony was the one who couldn't deal with some stuff he saw in a ville not far from Chu Lai. Tony had the Purple Heart and two Bronze Stars but volunteered to work in the mortuary so he wouldn't have to see things like that anymore.

Miles and me came home and played music, including gigs at Sharkey Bonano's Dream Room on Bourbon Street. Tony brought Vietnam back to New Orleans and carried it with him wherever he went. I wished Tony hadn't gotten messed up in the war and I wished he hadn't become a criminal, either. He was a good guy and had a good heart. So did Miles. That's why we were pals. Somehow, if we stayed together, we knew we'd never die.

Remember rumbles? When I was a kid, the gangs were Irish or Italian. Projects like the Iberville were all white, but the kids in them were the toughest I ever knew. They used to steal skulls out of the crypts in the St. Louis cemeteries and skate down North Villere Street with the skulls mounted on broomsticks. In the tenth grade a bunch of

them took my saxophone away from me on the streetcar.
Tony went into the project by himself, made a couple of
guys wet their pants, then walked into this kid's apartment
while the family was eating supper and came back out with
my sax. Nobody said squat.

Back in the 1950s and '60s, criminals had a funny status
in New Orleans. There were understandings between the
NOPD and the Italian crime family that ran all the vice.
Any hooker who cooperated with a Murphy sting on a john
in the Quarter got a bus ticket back to Snake's Navel, Texas.
Her pimp went off a rooftop. A guy who jack-rolled tourists
or old people got his wheels broken with batons and was
thrown out of a moving car by the parish line. Nobody was
sure what happened to child molesters. They never got
found.

But the city was a good place. You ever stroll across
Jackson Square in the early morning, when the sky was
pink and you could smell the salt on the wind and the coffee and pastry from the Café du Monde? Miles and me
used to sit in with Louis Prima and Sam Butera. That's no
jive, man. We'd blow until sunrise, then eat a bagful of hot
beignets and sip café au lait on a steel bench under the
palms while the sidewalk artists were setting up their easels
and paints in the square. The mist and sunlight in the trees
looked like cotton candy. That was before the city went
down the drain and before Miles and me went down the
drain with it.

Crack cocaine hit the projects in the early eighties.
Black kids all over the downtown area reminded me of the

characters in *Night of the Living Dead.* They loved 9mm automatics, too. The Gipper whacked federal aid to the city by half, and the murder rate in New Orleans became the highest in the United States. We got to see a lot of David Duke. He had his face remodeled with plastic surgery and didn't wear a bedsheet or a Nazi armband anymore, so the white-flight crowd treated him like Jefferson Davis and almost elected him governor.

New Orleans became a free-fire zone. Miles and me drifted around the Gulf Coast and smoked a lot of weed and pretended we were still jazz musicians. I'm not being honest here. It wasn't just weed. We moved right on up to the full-tilt boogie and joined the spoon-and-eyedropper club. Tony threw us both in a Catholic hospital and told this three-hundred-pound Mother Superior to beat the shit out of us with her rosary beads, one of these fifteen-decade jobs, if we tried to check out before we were clean.

But all these things happened before the storm hit New Orleans. After the storm passed, nothing Miles and Tony and me had done together seemed very important.

The color of the water is chocolate-brown, with a greenish-blue shine on the surface like gasoline, except it's not gasoline. All the stuff from the broken sewage mains has settled on the bottom. When people try to walk in it, dark clouds swell up around their chests and arms. I've never smelled anything like it.

The sun is a yellow flame on the brown water. It must be more than ninety-five degrees now. At dawn, I saw a black woman on the next street, one that's lower than mine, standing on top of a car roof. She was huge, with rolls of fat on her like a stack of inner tubes. She was wearing a purple dress that had floated up over her waist and she was waving at the sky for help. Miles rowed a boat from the bar he owns on the corner, and the two of us went over to where the car roof was maybe six feet underwater by the time we got there. The black lady was gone. I keep telling myself a United States Coast Guard chopper lifted her off. Those Coast Guard guys are brave. Except I haven't heard any choppers in the last hour.

Miles and me tie the boat to a vent on my roof and sit down on the roof's spine and wait. Miles takes out a picture of him and Tony and me together, at the old amusement park on Lake Pontchartrain. We're all wearing jeans and T-shirts and duck-ass haircuts, smiling, giving the camera the thumbs-up. You can't believe how handsome both Tony and Miles were, with patent-leather-black hair and Italian faces like Rudolph Valentino. Nobody would have ever believed Miles would put junk in his arm or Tony would come back from Vietnam with helicopter blades still thropping inside his head.

Miles brought four one-gallon jugs of tap water with him in his boat, which puts us in a lot better shape than most of our neighbors. This is the Ninth Ward of Orleans Parish. Only two streets away I can see the tops of palm trees sticking out of the water. I can also see houses that are completely covered. Last night I heard people beating the roofs from inside the attics in those houses. I have a feeling the sounds of those people will never leave my sleep, that the inside of my head is going to be like the inside of Tony's.

The church up the street is made out of pink stucco and has bougainvillea growing up one wall. The water is up to the little bell tower now, and the big cross in the breezeway with the hand-carved wooden Jesus on it is deep underwater. The priest tried to get everybody to leave the neighborhood, but a lot of people didn't have cars, or at least cars they could trust, and because it was still two days till payday, most people didn't have any money, either. So the priest said he was staying, too. An hour later the wind came off the Gulf and began to peel the face off South Louisiana.

This morning, I saw the priest float past the top of a live oak tree. He was on his stomach, his clothes puffed with air, his arms stretched out by his sides, like he was looking for something down in the tree.

The levees are busted and a gas main has caught fire under the water and the flames have set fire to the roof of a two-story house on the next block. Miles is pretty disgusted with the whole business. "When this is over, I'm moving to Arizona," he says.

"No, you won't," I say.

"Watch me."

"This is the Big Sleazy. It's Guatemala. We don't belong anywhere else."

He doesn't try to argue with that one. When we were kids we played with guys who had worked for King Oliver

and Kid Orey and Bunk Johnson, Miles on the drums, me
on tenor sax. Flip Phillips and Jo Jones probably didn't con-
sider us challenges to their careers, but we were respected
just the same. A guy who could turn his sticks into a white
blur at The Famous Door is going to move to a desert and
play "Sing, Sing, Sing" for the Gila monsters? That Miles
breaks me up.

His hair is still black, combed back in strings on his
scalp, the skin on his arms white as a baby's, puckered
more than it should be, but the veins are still blue and not
collapsed or scarred from the needlework we did on ourselves. Miles is a tough guy, but I know what he's thinking.
Tony and him and me started out together, then Tony got
into the life, and I mean into the life, man–drugs, whores,
union racketeering, loan-sharking, maybe even popping a
couple of guys. But no matter how many crimes he may
have committed, Tony held on to the one good thing in his
life, a little boy who was born crippled. Tony loved that little boy.

"Thinking about Tony?" I say.

"Got a card from him last week. The postmark was
Mexico City. He didn't sign it, but I know it's from him,"
Miles says.

He lifts his strap undershirt off his chest and wipes a
drop of sweat from the tip of his nose. His shoulders look
dry and hard, the skin stretched tight on the bone; they're
just starting to powder with sunburn. He takes a drink of
water from one of our milk jugs, rationing himself, swallow-
ing each sip slowly.

"I thought you said Tony was in Argentina."

"So he moves around. He's got a lot of legitimate busi-
nesses now. He's got to keep an eye on them and move
around a lot."

"Yeah, Tony was always hands-on," I say, avoiding his
eyes.

You know what death smells like? Fish blood that someone has buried in a garden of night-blooming flowers. Or a
field mortuary during the monsoon season in a tropical
country right after the power generators have failed. Or the
buckets that the sugar-worker whores used to pour into the
rain ditches behind their cribs on Sunday morning. If that
odor comes to you on the wind or in your sleep, you tend
to take special notice of your next sunrise.

I start looking at the boat and the water that goes to the
horizon in all directions. My butt hurts from sitting on the
spine of the house and the shingles burn the palms of my
hands. Somewhere up in Orleans Parish I know there's
higher ground, an elevated highway sticking up on pilings,
high-rise apartment buildings with roofs choppers can land
on. Miles already knows what I'm thinking. "Wait till dark,"
he says.

"Why?"

"There won't be as many people who want the boat,"
he says.

I look at him and feel ashamed of both of us.

A hurricane is supposed to have a beginning and an end. It tears the earth up, fills the air with flying trees and bricks and animals and sometimes even people, makes you roll up into a ball under a table and pray till drops of blood pop on your brow, then it goes away and lets you clean up after it, like somebody pulled a big prank on the whole town. But this one didn't work that way. It's killing in stages.

I see a diapered black baby in a tree that's only a green smudge under the water's surface. I can smell my neighbors in their attic. The odor is like a rat that has drowned in a bucket of water inside a superheated garage. A white guy floating by on an inner tube has a battery-powered radio propped on his stomach and tells us snipers have shot a policeman in the head and killed two Fish and Wildlife officers. Gangbangers have turned over a boat trying to rescue patients from Charity Hospital. The Superdome and the Convention Center are layered with feces and are without water or food for thousands of people who are seriously pissed off. A bunch of them tried to walk into Jefferson Parish and were turned back by cops who fired shotguns over their heads. The white-flight crowd doesn't need any extra problems.

The guy in the inner tube says a deer was on the second floor of a house on the next street and an alligator ate it.

That's supposed to be entertaining?

"You guys got anything to eat up there?" the guy in the inner tube asks.

"Yeah, a whole fucking buffet. I had it catered from Galatoire's right before the storm," Miles says to him.

That Miles.

Toward evening the sun goes behind the clouds and the sky turns purple and is full of birds. The Coast Guard choppers are coming in low over the water, the downdraft streaking a trough across the surface, the rescue guys swinging from cables like anyone could do what they do. They're taking children and old and sick people out first and flying without rest. I love those guys. But Miles and me both know how it's going to go. We've seen it before—the slick coming out of a molten sun, right across the canopy, automatic weapons fire whanging off the airframe, wounded grunts waiting in an LZ that North Vietnamese regulars are about to overrun. You can't get everybody home, Chuck. That's just the way it slides down the pipe sometimes.

A guy sitting on his chimney with Walkman ears on says the president of the United States flew over and looked down from his plane at us. Then he went on to Washington. I don't think the story is true, though. If the president was really in that plane, he would have landed and tried to find out what kind of shape we were in. He would have gone to the Superdome and the Convention Center and talked to the people there and told them the country was behind them.

The wind suddenly blows from the south, and I can smell salt and rain and the smell fish make when they're spawning. I think maybe I'm dreaming.

"Tony is coming," Miles says out of nowhere.

I look at his face, swollen with sunburn, the salt caked on his shoulders. I wonder if Miles hasn't pulled loose from his own tether.

"Tony knows where we are," he says. "He's got money and power and connections. We're the Mean Machine from Magazine. That's what he always said. The Mean Machine stomps ass and takes names."

For a moment I almost believe it. Then I feel all the bruises and fatigue, and the screaming sounds of the wind blowing my neighborhood apart drain out of me like black water sucking down through the bottom of a giant sink. My head sinks on my chest and I fall asleep, even though I know I'm surrendering my vigilance at the worst possible time.

I see Tony standing in the door of a Jolly Green, the wind flattening his clothes against his muscular physique. I see the Jolly Green coming over the houses, loading everyone on board, dropping bright yellow inflatable life rafts to people, showering water bottles and C-rats down to people who had given up hope.

But I'm dreaming. I wake up with a start. The sun is gone from the sky, the water still rising, the surface carpeted with trash. The painter to our boat hangs from the air vent, cut by a knife. Our boat is gone, our water jugs along with it.

≈≈≈

The night is long and hot, the stars veiled with smoke from fires vandals have set in the Garden District. My house is settling, window glass snapping from the frames as the floor buckles and the nails in the joists make sounds like somebody tightening piano wire on a wood peg.

It's almost dawn now. Miles is sitting on the ridge of the roof, his knees splayed on the shingles, like a human clothespin, staring at a speck on the southern horizon. The wind shifts, and I smell an odor like night-blooming flowers in a garden that has been fertilized with fish blood.

"Hey, Miles?" I say.

"Yeah?" he says impatiently, not wanting to be distracted from the speck on the horizon.

"We played with Louis Prima. He said you were as good as Krupa. We blew out the doors at the Dream Room with Johnny Scat. We jammed with Sharkey and Jack Teagarden. How many people can say that?"

"It's a Jolly Green. Look at it," he says.

I don't want to listen to him. I don't want to be drawn into his delusions. I don't want to be scared. But I am. "Where?" I ask.

"Right there, in that band of light between the sea and sky. Look at the shape. It's a Jolly Green. It's Tony, man, I told you."

The aircraft in the south draws nearer, like the evening star winking and then disappearing and then winking again. But it's not a Jolly Green. It's a passenger plane and it goes straight overhead, the windows lighted, the jet engines splitting the air with a dirty roar.

Miles's face, his eyes rolled upward as he watches the plane disappear, makes me think of John the Baptist's head on a plate.

"He's gonna come with an airboat. Mark my word," he says.

"The DEA killed him, Miles," I say.

"No, man, I told you. I got a postcard. It was Tony. Don't buy government lies."

"They blew him out of the water off Veracruz."

"No way, man. Not Tony. He got out of the life and had to stay off the radar. He's coming back."

I lie on my back, the nape of my neck cupped restfully on the roof cap, small waves rolling up my loins and chest like a warm blanket. I no longer think about the chemicals and oil and feces and body parts that the water may contain. I remind myself that we came out of primeval soup and that nothing in the earth's composition should be strange or objectionable to us. I look at the smoke drifting across the sky and feel the house jolt under me. Then it jolts again and I know that maybe Miles is right about seeing Tony, but not in the way he thought.

When I look hard enough into the smoke and the stars behind it, I see New Orleans the way it was when we were kids. I see the fog blowing off the Mississippi levee and pooling in the streets, the Victorian houses sticking out of the mist like ships on the Gulf. I see the green-painted streetcars clanging up and down the neutral ground on St. Charles and the tunnel of live oaks you ride through all the way down to the Carrollton District by the levee. The pink and purple neon tubing on the Katz & Besthoff drugstores glows like colored smoke inside the fog, and music is everywhere, like it's trapped under a big glass dome— the brass funeral bands marching down Magazine, old black guys blowing out the bricks in Preservation Hall, dance orchestras playing on hotel roofs along Canal Street.

That's the way it was back then. You woke in the morning to the smell of gardenias, the electric smell of the streetcars, chicory coffee, and stone that has turned green with lichen. The light was always filtered through trees, so it was never harsh, and flowers bloomed year-round. New Orleans was a poem, man, a song in your heart that never died.

I only got one regret. Nobody ever bothered to explain why nobody came for us. When Miles and me are way out to sea, I want to ask him that. Then a funny thing happens. Floating right along next to us is the big wood carving of Jesus on his Cross, from the stucco church at the end of my street. He's on his back, his arms stretched out, the waves sliding across his skin. The holes in his hands look just like the petals from the bougainvillea on the church wall. I ask him what happened back there.

He looks at me a long time, like maybe I'm a real slow learner.

"Yeah, I dig your meaning. That's exactly what I thought," I say, not wanting to show how dumb I am.

But considering the company I'm in—Jesus and Miles and Tony waiting for us somewhere up the pike—I got no grief with the world.

The stories included in this collection have previously appeared in a number of publications. "Winter Light" was published in *Epoch* (1992); "The Village" is excerpted from the novel *Burning Angel,* published by Hyperion (1995), and also appeared in *Image* (1995); "The Night Johnny Ace Died" was published in *Esquire* (2007); "Water People" was published in *Epoch* (1994); "Texas City, 1947" was published in *The Southern Review* (1991) and is excerpted from the novel *A Stained White Radiance,* published by Hyperion (1992); "Mist" was published in *The Southern Review* (2007); "A Season of Regret" was published in *Shenandoah* (2006); "The Molester" was published online in Amazon Shorts (2005); "The Burning of the Flag" was published in *Confrontation* (1995); "Why Bugsy Siegel Was a Friend of Mine" was published in *The Southern Review* (2005); "Jesus Out to Sea" was published in *Esquire* (2006).